VS

ZOMBIES
VS
ROBOTS

Z-Boyz in the Robot Graveyard

John Shirley

Z-Boyz in the Robot Graveyard

Illustrations by
Daniel Bradford

Edited by
Jeff Conner

IDW Publishing
San Diego, CA 2014

Dedications

For Jeff Conner, Richard Matheson and George Romero.
— John Shirley

For my wife, Krys. She lets me take time to draw gross stuff.
— Daniel Bradford

Vive Memor Leti

Editor/Designer: Jeff Conner

Associate Editor/tzvr: Chris Ryall
Associate Designer: Robbie Robbins

ZOMBIES vs. ROBOTS
Created by Ashley Wood & Chris Ryall

ISBN: 978-1-63140-008-7 17 16 15 14 1 2 3 4

Ted Adams, CEO & Publisher
Greg Goldstein, President & COO
Robbie Robbins, EVP/Sr. Graphic Artist
Chris Ryall, Chief Creative Officer/Editor-in-Chief
Matthew Ruzicka, CPA, Chief Financial Officer
Alan Payne, VP of Sales
Dirk Wood, VP of Marketing
Lorelei Bunjes, VP of Digital Services
Jeff Webber, VP of Digital Publishing & Business Development

IDWPUBLISHING.com

Become our fan on Facebook **facebook.com/idwpublishing**
Follow us on Twitter **@idwpublishing**
Check us out on YouTube **youtube.com/idwpublishing**

Illustrationen von Daniel Bradförd

Z-BOYZ
IN THE
ROBOT GRAVEYARD

She was tall and slim, wearing shorts and a tank top, goggles, her black hair cut short.

FOOD CHAIN

"Cold metal, got to be
Skeleton of the free..."
— *Iggy Pop*

1.

KEESHA DRIVING THE DIRT buggy, Ruben literally riding shotgun, Lyle in the back, they crossed the desert and found the robot graveyard exactly where the old guidance satellite said it'd be. Keesha's goggles were almost browned out with the dust of the Arizona wasteland, so she had to wipe them with a wetted thumb to be sure. Yeah, there it was, a big old junkyard of robot and automated tractor parts, shining like pirate treasure in the mid-morning sun. And it *was* treasure, a techno-trove of parts nobody built anymore, pieces she could cobble into working guardians.

They could see great heaps of steel carapaces and connectives rising over the electrified barbed wire fence, metal and glass glancing out thin spears of reflected sun. Jutting three stories over the fenced lot was a square-edged watch tower of some kind, meshed concrete over a metal frame. She couldn't see anyone in its window.

The gate in the scrapyard's outer fence was wide open. And that wasn't how it should be. Anyone that friendly was probably dead.

But maybe that made things simpler.

They'd driven all the way from Base 23, across the desert, night and day, staying clear of roads when possible, trying to decrease the chance of running into braineaters, and they were almost out of fuel. Their only choice was to hope the place wasn't overrun…

Keesha spotted a few shamblers off to their right, maybe an eighth mile to the east, unmistakable even at this distance. The dirt buggy would reach the dump—but then what? The gate was open so good chance there were zombies inside. Getting lost in a maze of metal odds and ends with an unknown number of voracious, frustrated braineaters was not part of her plan.

Keesha slowed down as they approached the gate, wondering if there were landmines in the dirt—the open gate could be a way to lure the unwary, trigger a mine. Blow up a traveler, steal their stuff. Some of the more hardcore survivors were capable of it.

No. The zombies would have set off the landmines by now.

She drove slowly up to the gate…almost stopping…not ready to enter the place yet…

"What are you waiting for?" Ruben asked, spitting dust and shifting the shotgun from his left hand to his right; he wedged its stock butt against his right hip so he could fire if a zombie rushed them. He was a sallow fat-cheeked guy, about forty, in greasy jeans and yellowing T-shirt, with two days' growth of dark beard and a sunburned bald spot on his head.

Keesha was a contrast. She was tall and slim, wearing shorts and a tank top, goggles, her black hair cut short.

"Come on," Ruben said, "Christ, more'n a hundred miles trying to get here, let's fucking go in."

Her brother Lyle leaned forward. "She's doing the smart thing, dude, just chill." Lyle was a little younger and shorter than his sister, but the same cocoa color; he wore blue coveralls turning yellow with dust; his corn-rowed black hair was dust coated too.

"Not sure I want to just plunge into this fucking place," Keesha said.

"We got to hope there's fuel here, anyway," Ruben pointed out. "What else we going to do, at this point?"

"I know. I'm just...trying to see."

They couldn't see anything move inside; they heard the wind whining in the fence wires, and nothing else.

"Lyle—" she began.

"I'm ready," he said, cocking the pistol. He often anticipated what she was going to say.

Keesha took a deep breath and drove slowly through the gate, squinting against the glare of light off metal and plastic and glass. They drove into the shadow of the watchtower.

She shut off the engine, pulled her assault rifle from its clamp next to the gearshift, and the first of the zombies came shuffling around the corner of a pile of random machine parts.

The braineater wore shapeless rags, was missing his lower jaw and one eye. The zombie's right leg dragged some, and that slowed him down so it was easy to drop the muzzle of the assault rifle and squeeze off a short burst—the zombie's head exploded, black-red blood flying up and back to glitter in the sunlight before he fell, writhing in a second death.

Keesha turned when Ruben fired a round, off to his right; she saw he'd cut a zombie in a bloody party dress almost in half. Sawn through at close range by the eight gauge, the zombie's upper half sagged one way, its lower the other, but it was still connected by entrails and flesh, still moving, trying to crawl toward them. Lyle aimed carefully and shot her in the head.

Lyle murmured, "I always feel like I've done something nice for somebody when I shoot one of them in the head. I mean, something nice for the zombie..."

They heard the sounds of other braineaters, somewhere in the junkyard. Groaning, hissing, clunking into obstacles.

"We got no choice but to clear the place out," Keesha said, looking around for more targets. "Gunshots will bring more of 'em from the desert so I better close that gate. We don't have enough fuel to make any kind of serious run for it. You guys cover me." She got out of the dirt buggy.

But Lyle was already jumping out of the back. "I'll close the gate, you stay near to Ruben," he said. "Doesn't seem like the fence electricity's going..."

Lyle was trying to protect her but she was better with a gun than he was. Really, it should be her. Too late to insist now, he was running across the open ground up to the gate...checking for electricity. The power wasn't flowing so Lyle started to close the gate manually. The gate closed slowly, as he tugged it along, creaking from right to left on a rusty wheel.

"Keesha, behind you!" Ruben barked. She turned, fired from the hip before seeing what kind of zombie it was—it didn't matter anyway, a braineater's a braineater. It was a naked kid, as it happened, or had been a kid, maybe twelve years old, face and hair matted in old dried blood and flecks of rotting flesh, like he'd stuck his whole head in somebody's guts, which he probably had—her rounds missed him except one in the forehead, and he staggered backward, tipped over, fell flat.

"There you go, kid," she said. "You're welcome."

Ruben was firing at another, a squat Mestizo zombie; he used up two shotgun shells before the third took the top of the shambler's head off.

Keesha spun at a yell from the gate and saw that her brother had it shut—but a cyanotic arm poked through, in the narrow space between gate and fence pole, the zombie outside the gate grabbing Lyle's wrist. Before she could move, Lyle fired the pistol through the crack between the gate and the fence, twice, and the grip went slack. The mottled gray hand withdrew. Lyle closed a lock on the gate and turned toward her, grinning, and waving. There was blood running down his hand, curling around his wrist.

NO MORE LIVING DEAD in the robot graveyard, but there were still some outside the fence. Keesha was surprised there were so many of them this far from a population center, but Ruben said they were probably from a little town he'd seen on the map, small place built around a truck stop about eight miles off.

They waited, but no other zombies came at them. They searched the junkyard, found only the remains of a coyote in one corner of the lot, its head cracked open, brains gnawed out long ago, most of its flesh stripped away by rats and insects.

They called out, and searched—couldn't find the guy who'd set up the junkyard, though he'd been reported alive and open for business just two months earlier.

Under the watchtower they found a bunker, a fifteen-by-twenty foot, low-ceilinged underground concrete room; along one wall were plastic shelves holding crates of food, a box of shotgun shells, and a crate of medical supplies. The food, shells and medical goods made the trip here worthwhile, if nothing else—and in one corner, by a cluttered workbench, was the partly finished body of a preservation bot: the rudiments of an artificial man standing, as if casually waiting, in a rack against one wall. Keesha inspected it, found the nanocrystaline brain in the aluminum skull fully installed, and the limbs and torso nearly complete. Nearby was a crate of synthetic skins to sheath it with, in several shades.

"What the fuck is that, some kind of android?" Ruben asked, addressing Keesha because she was the geek here. Ruben seemed particularly surly now; kept stealing narrow-eyed looks at Lyle as they checked out the bunker.

"Looks like a pres-bot," Keesha replied. "Some survivalist types homebuild 'em, or try to—they're crazy complicated, real Kurzweil stuff. Supposedly they can imprint an entire personality, memories and all, right from your brain. Guess the guy who ran this place was fixing to be immortal. That unit over there by the bot probably copies neural patterns, does the transfer. Took a tutorial on preservation bots once when I—"

"That ain't going to help us out with our mission," Ruben growled. "Base council said we were only to get parts for base protection. Food's a good thing to find—but you think you can locate what we need here for the guardians? We need to get this done and get the hell back, fast as we can. Like right now." He glanced at Lyle again.

"I have to do an inventory," she said, shrugging. "Should be able to hack into the junkyard's accounts computer—see what's listed, probably do a search for the relevant specs and narrow it to—"

"Okay, cool, fine, I get it, you're really smart and all, but the real question is—what's your *brother* doing there, right about now?" Ruben nodded toward Lyle, who was kneeling by the crates of freeze-dried dinners. "What exactly…?"

"Most of this food is really bogus protein fabrication," Lyle muttered, ignoring Ruben, as he usually did—as most people did. "It'll feed us, though. I think there's some real peas in this one."

Ruben ogled Lyle and shook his head. "Early stages..."

"Ruben—what the hell you yappin' about?" Keesha asked, her fingers tightening on the rifle. She wasn't sure why she was shifting her grip on that rifle—not consciously. But some part of her knew, already. So her fingers knew...

"I mean," Ruben said, "He got...wait." He used his fingers to wipe the thick dust from his teeth—his teeth were still yellow after the dust came off. He spat on the concrete floor. "He got bit on the arm out there."

That got Lyle's attention. He stood up, turned toward Ruben. "You should've worn a hat on the trip here, dude. Fried your brains through that bald spot."

"See there?" Ruben chuckled nastily. "He's thinking about fried brains!"

"That supposed to be humorous?" Keesha asked.

"Maybe not! We got to tie him up and watch for symptoms. Only I'm not getting near him. You got to do it. Was you, I'd knock him out first."

"The fuck," Lyle said, shaking his head. "Hello? I'm right here, dude! I look like I'm a zombie walking around and biting on people?"

"It's only a matter of time, and not much at that. I can see that cut on your arm there, boy."

"I got that from the fence, trying to yank it. There was a razor wire along the edges—"

"Maybe. But it's a hole in your skin and you shot a zombie almost point blank. I saw a lot of blood on your arm. All of it yours? What if you got Z-blood in that cut?"

"None of its blood got on me!"

"You don't know that and *we* don't know that and I'm sure as shit not taking any chances." He pointed his shotgun at Lyle.

"Ruben," Keesha said, through clenched teeth. "Put that fucking shotgun down right this second."

Ruben looked at her—then back at Lyle who was starting toward him. Lyle was reaching for the muzzle of Ruben's shotgun.

Ruben tensed, and the shotgun roared. Lyle was kicked off his feet, flung back, arms flapping as acrid gunsmoke choked the small bunker.

Once more, Keesha's fingers decided what to do before she did. She squeezed the trigger on the assault rifle and the burst smashed through Ruben's throat, splashing the concrete wall behind him with blood as he spun and fell, gurgling.

Keesha dropped the rifle, rushed to Lyle, fell to her knees beside him, tears blurring her eyes. He was alive but the shotgun blast had taken him just under the ribs on the left side. He was gushing blood, shaking, eyes rolling back.

"Keesha...oh...I don't know...I'm scared..."

She jumped up, stepped over the inert Ruben, snatched the nearest box of bandages from the shelf, tore it open as she hurried back to Lyle, and got the wound staunched. But by the time she was done he was shaking, lips turning blue. She took his pulse—it was feeble and intermittent.

"Keesha...bury me...head shot...don't let them..."

"You're not going to die, Lyle."

But she knew he was. She looked at the preservation bot. She looked at Lyle. She looked at the cerebral copy machine...

• • •

2.

FIVE MONTHS LATER.

The whole world was made of metal, that early morning. The sun, rising through gray haze in the east, off to Keesha's left, cast the desert plains around the robot graveyard in a metallic gray-blue light.

Much of this place was in fact metal. Keesha was up high, standing on the steel platform with Lyle2—the cybernetic copy of her brother Lyle—looking out over the ragged, chunky metal vista of the robot graveyard; the blue-tinged desert beyond. They were standing in the little room at the top of the watchtower. Her assault rifle was nearby, leaning on the metal bulkhead under the window.

She hadn't been able to sleep—sometimes it made her feel better to come up here and pot-shoot some zombies. She was a pretty good long-distance shot by now. She liked to keep them off the electric fence. If enough of them piled up on it their main defense might short out. She'd worked hard getting the power flowing through it again.

It was still chilly from the night, and her thin bare legs were goose-pimpling. She wore shorts and a hoodie and sandals, and her long legs were exposed. "You should put on some more clothes, Sis," said Lyle2, seeing her shiver, saying it just the way Lyle would have. The synthetic voice was only slightly off. She glanced at him—in the shadowy sniper's aerie atop the watchtower the robot's silhouette was just like Lyle's. She could pretend, for a moment, that her younger brother was still alive, standing right beside her.

Grow up, she told herself. *You're almost thirty. Lyle's dead and Lyle2 is just a talking wax museum replica.*

Keesha looked back out at the gray daybreak, wondering where she'd find the parts she needed for the guardians—the defense robots that might save what was left of her family, her few friends…and Base 23.

The cybernetic scrapyard was eighteen square acres of metal and plastic parts, big and small parts, most of them randomly tumbled about, some loosely organized according to type. The softly rising wind whined over the fence, brought the scents of mesquite and sage and dust. And rotting human flesh. She could pick out the shapes of widely separated saguaro, out there, stark as crude pictoglyphs, and the occasional short, spiny tree—and between cacti and the trees, things were moving: the living dead, shambling toward the robot graveyard; toward Keesha and Lyle2. Too far away, as yet, for a good head shot. The unsteady silhouettes of the shamblers cast stretched-out, attenuated shadows east to west. Sometimes, when the braineaters hesitated, in this post-dawn dimness, they looked like saguaro themselves—and then the apparent cactus would take a step, and rake its arms at the sky.

The high-voltage electric fence, powered up now, kept the walking dead at bay—in the desert around the robot graveyard was another kind of graveyard, a ring of sprawled, well-cooked electrocuted zombies, brains boiled out of their eyeballs, bodies inert, but some still trailing smoke. Other still-moving shamblers had fingers charred to the bone.

"I should never have come here," Keesha said. "'Cause I'll never get out of here. Big mistake bringing that idiot Ruben."

"You did get a guardian built."

"No way to get it home! Doesn't store enough power to get itself across the desert. And we would travel too slow, anyway. Thought there'd be a truck or…"

"Speaking of vehicles, Sis—I do believe I hear one…an aerial vehicle," Lyle2 said, peering out to the north.

"Really? I don't hear it. And I don't see it."

"I'm definitely hearing something out there, something like a helicopter."

"*Where,* dammit?" She was feeling more trapped with every day they spent in this place. A plane, a chopper—that could be a way out.

"North. It's flying low…" The Lyle bot had better hearing, better senses in general, than a human. "Too low." He was turning his head, slowly, like a radar antenna. "Coming from… Oh. I've lost it. The sound stopped…"

"Shit." Keesha took the binoculars off their hook, scanned the low rolling desert. "I still don't see it."

"I suspect it crashed. The sound cut off real sudden…"

They waited. Time passed and she imagined zombies lunging at some poor broken bastard's crashed chopper, moving in to chew him up alive…

Then a dark human shape came clambering over the fence; dropping down, scurrying to take cover behind the hulk of a shattered agribot.

They saw him only as a sketchy man-shape at first, because he was coming down in an underlit corner of the lot, about thirty yards away, just inside the electrified wire.

"Fucking zombie, dammit, how'd it get over the fence—" Keesha grabbed her assault rifle, stepped to find a sniper position. "Power must be down."

"No, I can hear the fence humming," Lyle2 said.

Then she saw the dim figure moving down the aisle cleared between piles of junk; between steel carapaces and rusting hard drives, coming their way. "Smells our blood from there…"

She sighted on its head…

"Wait!" Lyle2 said. "I zoomed in on it—better look at this." He turned to her, stuck his hand out, palm upward. His palm, with its fairly realistic synthetic skin, lit up in a little square showing the digital photo he'd taken with his robotic eyes: A man in a helmet, leather jacket, pistol in a gloved hand. "He doesn't look like a zombie."

"Didn't move like one either," Keesha admitted. "Could be a roamer, though. Most of 'em are psychos." But she lowered the rifle—and called out, "You! Down in the junkyard! Come toward the tower, slowly, hands in the air! Keep that gun pointed at the sky!"

Not quite a full minute passed before the man stepped into view about twenty yards away, coming out from behind a pile of debris, his hands up.

"Drop the pistol!" she ordered. "And open that helmet!"

He seemed to hesitate, then dropped the pistol. He flicked up the helmet visor.

"I'm no braineater!" the stranger yelled, his voice hoarse. "I'm not a raider either! Hold your fire!"

"You can lower your hands but keep them where I can see 'em and come closer!"

She turned to Lyle2. "Let's go. You take the rifle."

The assault rifle strapped over his shoulder, the preservation bot stepped to the hatch that opened to the outside front of the tower. He slid neatly down the metal ladder; Keesha quickly followed, mouth dry with excitement.

At the bottom of the ladder she turned to see the stranger walking toward them, a look of wry annoyance on his long, pale face, his motorcycle helmet tucked under his arm. He had a thatch of short yellow hair, arched brows and a whimsical mouth. He was as tall and slim as she was, and not a bad-looking guy, in a pallid sort of way. Keesha liked the amusement in his blue eyes. She was used to seeing desperation.

"How did you get past the electric fence?" she asked. "The power down?" That was a worrisome thought.

The stranger shook his head. "I have insulated gloves and boots, what else? Stood on my bike to reach the top. Braineaters snapping at my goddamn heels when I went over."

She nodded. "We heard a motorcycle. Thought it was a helicopter."

"Probably that *was* the helicopter. This bike's tuned quiet so it doesn't attract the fucking zombies."

"You some government operative? Where'd you get a motorcycle?"

He shook his head. "I'm strictly a civilian. Restored an old Robinson 22 fixed-wing. Fucking thing bleeds fuel though; think it's leaking. Ran out a quarter mile out from here. Crash landed, pretty much wrecked the chopper. It's not going anyplace. Got a rack for an old Kawasaki crotch rocket on the back..." He shrugged. "I jumped on and got rolling right before the braineaters closed in. Shot two in the head and rode through the gap."

"Sounds real intrepid and all," she said skeptically. "Where were you on your way to?"

"Coming right here." He looked at her bare legs. "You wanta tell me your name?"

"I guess. I'm Keesha. This is Lyle2."

The stranger looked at Lyle2. "Is Lyle there a preservation bot?"

Lyle2 pretended to bow a little, like a guy in an old Japanese movie, and said, "Lyle2. At your service, dude." Which was pretty close to what Lyle himself would've said and done, him with his nerdy sense of humor. The personality overlay was erratic, though. His mind was a copy, and only a partial copy, using an extrapolation program to fill in the blanks.

The stranger nodded. "Curson. I'm Curt Curson. So..." He grinned. "Let's have the next question. Aren't you going to ask *why* I was coming here?"

"Yeah, well, I was kind of hoping they missed me at the base and sent you out. I don't know you, and I think I know everyone there. But I've been here five months so I figured maybe they got some fresh blood in."

"What base is that?"

"Base 23." She pointed. "A long ways off in that direction."

He shook his head. "Never heard of Base 23. I came from Tucson."

"Curson from Tucson?" Lyle2 asked, trying to appear amused, though his smiles didn't work very well.

"Yeah. South of Tucson really. We got a little community there—where that privatized prison complex used to be. When the complex went out of business, they left it empty."

"You live in a *prison*?"

"It's not a prison anymore. Except o'course the zombies make it one, in a way. We can't get out much. Running low on food. No warbots. Living on green beans that taste like the can—supplemented with feral cats and dogs and the occasional coyote or vulture. Vulture's not bad if you cook it right."

"How many are you?"

"Near a hundred. What's the deal with Base 23?"

"It's a military base, set up for refugees. FEMA/DoD stuff. About two hundred of us there. Two hundred left, I mean. No warbots, either. They left…to kill zombies." She couldn't help smirking.

"Better off without 'em, I say. Two hundred, huh? That's a lot. Just the pair of you here? I didn't think anyone'd be around, except maybe a guard bot. How'd you get the fence juiced up? Solar?"

"Yeah. Pumped up with a transformer sequence, voltage multiplier, some diodes with superconducting components…and a whole lotta big batteries from the junkyard."

"Nice. I heard this place was a robot graveyard. Why I'm here, right? Cyberparts. Those and food."

She nodded slowly. "Scavenging." There was nothing pejorative in her tone. Scavenging was how most people survived, now. It was almost everyone's profession.

Curt smiled, with just one side of his mouth. "Fresh robotics are hard to find now. Saw this dump listed in an old flash drive, so…" He looked at Lyle2 as if imagining the spare parts in him, then back at Keesha. "You scavenging too—for whatever?"

Keesha snorted. "Always—but there's something else too. I'm building some stuff. I've got a definite purpose. Thought I did, anyway, before I got stuck here. Vehicle got trashed, zombies started circling the place. We leave on foot, we're zombie food."

"What are you living on here, speaking of food?"

Should she tell him? He might kill her for the food. Zombies weren't the only killers out there. But he was the first flicker of a way out they'd had in months.

"Come on, I'll show you the eats." Even as she said it, she thought, *I shouldn't trust him.*

Only, she had to. Except for this interloper all she had were zombies and robots…

"FREEZE-DRIED, HUH?" Curt murmured, as he looked over the remainder of her stores; maybe four months worth for one person, five if she really pushed it.

They were in the concrete bunker, her and Curt and Lyle2, a basement room beneath the watchtower. The low-ceilinged room smelled of dust and mildew. A naked bulb glared close overhead.

"Freeze-dried is what we got," Keesha said. "Guy who owned the place was some kind of survivalist, probably had it stored up a long time. When we got here the gate was open, a few zombies wandering around—we figure he went outside the perimeter to repair something and got overrun. Couldn't have been too long before we came or the roamers would've ransacked the place."

"Not that we've seen any," Lyle2 said. "Not even a raider."

"How about water?" Curt asked.

"There's an underground river—he pumped it up from there, and filtered it. It's even possible to take a shower. There's a septic tank, too."

"It could be," Lyle2 put in, with a tilt of his fairly realistic head, "that one of the zombies we shot when we got here, six months ago, used to be the owner."

Curt grunted, opening a box to look at freeze-dried protein dinners. "Good of him to supply you, accidentally or not. You come here alone—I mean, with Lyle2 here?"

"No." She kept her voice steady as she went on. "I had my brother with me and another guy, Ruben. And Ruben thought my brother was going zombie. He panicked about him—he shot Lyle..."

Curt looked curiously at her. "So you shot Ruben? And then made Lyle2 here?"

She nodded. "The gear was right here in the bunker."

Keesha swallowed and sat on a folding chair in front of the workbench. "They were out there in the yard for a couple of weeks under a tarp. I just couldn't deal with burying him. Lyle2 here did it for me. 'Course after Lyle died I shot him through the brains to keep him from turning into a..." She licked her lips. Her mouth felt dry. "I mean, I didn't know if he was infected like Ruben said. Just couldn't take any chances..."

He nodded. "Sure. And Ruben?"

"Tossed the asshole over the wall to feed the braineaters. Least they're good for something."

He laughed dryly. "I'll remember not to mess with you! You come in that busted dirt buggy I saw out there?"

"Yeah. We discovered it wasn't very effective against massing zombies—didn't have enough fuel to get far anyhow."

He tossed a package of freeze-dried food in the air and caught it. "So—any chance of some breakfast? Haven't eaten since yesterday."

"Okay." She pointed a firm finger at him. "But I'm not saying you can take more than that one meal. You know how it is. We'd have to talk about that."

He nodded, not seeming worried about it. "Fine. One meal. And we'll talk."

"Let's try the so-called ham dinner there. It tastes like dirt with a little salt and gravy but... better than nothing."

"I'll heat it up for you," Lyle2 said. "It's the only part of eating I can participate in..."

They ate in silence, sitting on crates, using plastic spoons to eat the gunky brown slop in the little plastic trays. Afterward, Lyle2 poured some drinking water into mason jars, then went to his corner of the room to plug in for awhile.

"Gonna have my own chow," he said, plugging a jack into his hip. His face blanked as he went into recharge mode.

Keesha tossed her empty tray into a small metal trash barrel. She was starting to relax around Curt. He hadn't asked for his gun back, which was a good sign. She still had her rifle within reach but he didn't seem the least bit hostile. It was like they'd grown up together—maybe because they recognized something in one another. They were both engineers. *Geeks*, some said. She preferred to say *technologically talented.*

"What you looking for," she asked at last, noticing him checking out her legs again. Hastily adding, "I mean—in the 'robot graveyard.' Just anything usable?"

"Our guard systems are breaking down. I've got a new idea I want to try out. Not enough parts for it. Maybe close to the same thing you're looking for. Maybe I can help you—get us all out of here. You want to show me these—things you were working on?"

She didn't hesitate. She felt almost drunk on hope.

"THEY'RE GUARDIANS," KEESHA SAID excitedly. "My design—more like mobile garbage disposals; to *dispose* of zombies without expending ammunition. Just do the job fast and dirty. We need something that'll kill a lot of shamblers fast without ammo so we can clear the way for food forays—like most everyone else. One problem is keeping these babies clean…the grinders are gonna splatter blood, infectious zombie blood, and it'll get all over the mechanism so the risk of contact with it…"

"Yeah, I see," Curt said, with his lopsided grin. "Sweet idea."

She was relieved he hadn't ridiculed the idea, like a lot of people at the base had.

They were in the open-air work yard, standing in the shadow of the finished guardian. Switched off and inert but ominous anyway, the robot was about nine feet high, its columnar legs set into flexible treads capable of climbing stairs, working its way over small obstacles. The guardian was a tall, bulky, faceted wedge of gray metal, its swiveling bucket-shaped head fitted with an old-fashioned video camera. Optical sensors ringed its upper chest giving it 360 degrees of system-fused digital perception. Its arms were modified construction lifters, things of massive joints and pistons and pincers; its torso was fitted with two sets of knife-sized external disposal slashers, looking like boat props—or blades from a giant juice blender.

"We were short on ammo, so I thought, why waste bullets?" Keesha said proudly.

Curt nodded, his mouth making a moue of appreciation. "Smart. And you had guts to come here, just you and this Ruben and Lyle. I've gotta admire that."

She licked her lips and looked away. She liked the attention and wasn't sure of it, at once. "You don't have to admire anything. I just wanted to explain the concept. I got a lot of help from Lyle2—couldn't have built it without him. My specs, but he did all the welding, lotta heavy lifting."

"All these months here, just you and..."

"Lyle2's not bad company. But yeah, it's not like having real people to talk to."

"Scanning your brother's personality, putting it in a bot—that's impressive too. I mean, that tech's been out there but not many people know how to use it."

"I was feeling pretty intensely...you know, focused. I was going to be all alone and...my brother..." Keesha looked away. She didn't want to show any weakness around this guy. He was still a stranger to her. She finished lamely, "He was always there. I just couldn't...not have him around at all."

"That bootleg pres-bot—does it really seem like, you know...him?"

"Sometimes—and sometimes it's like his ghost. But maybe that's just because I've been alone so long."

He looked at Lyle2. "Doesn't seem human to me. Just a quality DIY robot, pretty good synth-tex skin, smooth movements, but—his eyes don't blink, his voice doesn't sound natural, not quite..."

"He's all I've had for company. Him and the guardian." She patted the metal skin of the zombie killer. "My big baby here."

Curt grinned. "Cute baby. So—what power source, what kind of CPU? You using a quantum-cloud chip or what in this baby of yours?"

They talked tech for almost an hour, enjoying the geek communion, looking over the guts of the unfinished second guardian, until he said, abruptly, "You had a test run with the finished unit?"

"I've directed it around the yard. Cut up some boxes with it...It controls pretty good; got an autonomous program that seems to work."

"You did a brilliant job with those sensors. But I meant—you haven't tested the guardian on the braineaters?"

"No. No, I haven't figured out...I mean, I could hose it off but if one drop of their blood stays on it and I get it on me..."

"Yeah. Still. You ought to know if it works or not. How about you try it out, I'll wear gloves and hose it off, be really careful?"

Keesha found she wanted to impress him. She knew that somewhere in the back of her mind she was making the same calculation most unattached women had to make, now, when they met any man: *Is he suitable for making kids? Will he think I'm suitable for him?* Because there were few men to go around, and everyone felt a piercing urgency to make children; to keep the human race going. Despite everything, despite the horror the world had become—or because of it.

"Okay," she said. "Let's put some flex sealant over these couplings and on the manifold seams, try to keep blood from getting inside..."

It was mid-afternoon before they had it set up for the trial run. The day had gotten hot; the sky was pale blue. Occasionally they heard the bubbling sizzle and inhuman shriek of a convulsing zombie frying on the fence outside.

"Where'd you get that old remote control box?" Curt asked, as she prepared to start the guardian up.

She grinned. "Shell and the antenna, they're from a remote control toy tank. Least twenty years old. Guts are a bit slicker now..."

She aimed the antenna, which probably wasn't necessary, and flicked the *On* switch. The guardian straightened up like a man asleep trying to come to attention, its steel joints creaking.

Lyle2 joined them, strolling in from his perimeter check, carrying his shotgun strapped over his shoulder. Keesha realized she'd forgotten her assault rifle; had leaned it against the frame of a junk shelf, which was being too careless altogether with a new guy around.

Lyle2 had a pistol held loosely in his hand. "Should I give him his gun back?" he asked, looking at her.

She glanced at Curt, who was crouched down studying the articulation of the guardian's treads.

Keesha decided she had to go with her gut on this. "Yeah. Go ahead."

Lyle2 flipped the gun around, offering it butt-first to Curt.

Curt straightened up, took the gun without a word, and stuck it in his waistband. "Lyle, we're gonna take the guardian for a test drive. You'll want to stand by with the assault rifle in case anything gets by the guardian at the front gate..."

Keesha frowned. Curt was giving her robot orders. But then, maybe it was natural—Curt was human, Lyle2 wasn't. A robot was designed to be subordinate. At least the guy was nice enough to call him Lyle and not "robot" as some people would've.

Lyle2 looked at her with a fair simulation of "you want me to do this?" in his expression—and she nodded. He took his shotgun off his shoulder strap, held it ready for business, and started for the front gate.

A CLOUD DRIFTED OVER the sun, drawing a sickly membrane of dull gray shadow over the desert outside the robot graveyard...

...Where four zombies came clambering over the moraine of mummified corpses, coming toward the open gate; coming toward Keesha, Lyle2 and Curt, standing just inside.

Vultures circled closely over the shamblers, almost within reach. Keesha figured they must be confused by zombies—by things that smelled quite dead but kept walking.

A particularly enterprising vulture swooped down and lit on the shoulder of a zombie in a highway patrolman's uniform, began pecking away the officer's right eye. The zombie snarled and smacked at the vulture; the vulture clung and dug its beak deep into an eye socket, right into brain matter. The zombie cop grabbed convulsively at the vulture and fell over, taking the squawking bird down with it, in a flurry of black feathers....

The other zombies never looked back. They kept moving, twitchily but inexorably, toward the gate.

Keesha had the shotgun on a strap over one shoulder, the remote control in her hand. Lyle2 had the rifle, Curt clutched his pistol.

Growling, murmuring wordlessly, four of the living dead moved steadily toward the motionless guardian at the gate; farther off, others trotted and staggered, coming gradually closer in a kind of zombie Brownian motion. Still others stumbled in circles, shaking their heads like dogs with ear mites.

The four zombies closest to the open gate, working their way toward Keesha and Lyle2 and Curt, had once been two women and two men. One of them, the fat man in farmer's overalls, looked almost fresh, like he'd died quite recently. Keesha wondered how he had stayed fat, with food so hard to come by. Another zombie had been a housekeeper, judging by her uniform. She still had the white shoes on, though they were splashed brown with dried blood. A third zombie, once a black man, wore a hospital orderly's white coat, and blue pants, but his lacerated feet were bloodily bare. The fourth had been a middle-aged woman. She was naked now but for a gore-spattered brassiere; her skin was beet-red, peeling, burned by the sun, her dyed blonde hair warped and puffed in a cartoonish mock of its original perm. They all had their heads ducked a bit, eyes focused on their prey, like drunken cats about to pounce.

About ten yards off, the fat man blunderingly stepped through the moldering chest of a headless zombie's remains, foot crushing through the brittle rib cage, so that dried-out guts puffed up in a brown cloud like spores from a fungus. The fat zombie snarled and pulled its foot free…

"All those bodies laying around outside almost stopped me trying to come in here," Curt said. "Not a welcoming sight. Then I figured out they were zombie roadkill…"

"We shut off the fence from time to time and shove the bodies off it," Lyle2 said. "Coyotes and vultures drag some of them away. Wonder if there are zombie coyotes…never seen any."

"Ready, Keesha?" Curt asked, drawing the pistol from his waistband as the four closest zombies picked up speed—as they always did when they got close. Getting ready to charge.

"Let's do it," she said, and flicked the little joystick on the remote so that the guardian in front of her rolled forward, angled toward the four zombies.

She hoped to Jesus it worked. A rush by a throng of zombies could easily overwhelm two guns…

"Better hold it there," Curt said. "Wait for them to come to it."

She nodded and pulled back on the joystick to stop the guardian about four yards out from the fence, then thumbed the *Attack Response* button.

The guardian stopped; its arms creaked and twitched. Then it seemed inert. But she could hear its works humming from here.

The zombies seemed to sniff at the enormous robot as they approached—and started past it, sensing the guardian was fleshless.

The hulking robot reacted the moment they got within reach, its arms hooking out, gathering the two nearest zombies into its embrace, a process that took half a second. The blades were already whirring when it clutched the fat man and the naked woman close. Blood fanned out to the front and side of the guardian, each arc of red about fifteen feet in diameter. The zombies in its grip squealed and gnashed helplessly. The other two zombies hesitated, confused by the spray of blood.

Keesha flicked another button and the whirring stopped, the blood ceased flying, and the big robot turned toward her, displaying the remains of its victims. There were no heads, nothing visible above the waist but shreds, the lower bodies oozing from its grip to flop onto the ground.

"Nice!" Curt enthused, as he aimed his pistol at the still-moving zombie in the housekeeper dress. "Keep it turned off while it's facing us!" He fired three times, the third shot nailing his target in the forehead. The zombie spun, staggered, and fell.

Lyle2 was aiming the assault rifle at the erstwhile orderly which growled bubblingly as it charged. The preservation bot fired with effortless precision—the top of the zombie's head blew away and it fell face down, just outside the gate frame.

"Shit," Curt said, "I wasted two bullets. But damn, your guardian is a good boy! Churned them up with beautiful efficiency."

Keesha shrugged, watching the other zombies. The braineaters were still a ways off but starting more urgently toward them. "Never doubted it. Problem is, I'd have to build two more to make a real dent in all these zombies out here—and a guardian uses up a lot of power. They'd run out of power before they cleared a good path for us. Solar power takes too long to charge. Then there's the maintenance problem, the blood spray—you saw how far it splashes. Be pretty easy to mess up and get bathed in zombie blood. And there's transporting the guardians. Lyle—get that one."

Lyle2 was already aiming at the zombie leading the pack—this one was a tall bald black braineater; its lips were missing, torn away. It made a gobbling sound as it came on—which cut off as Lyle2 shot it through the neck, and then again in the head.

"It squirmed and made me miss my first shot," he said. "We're wasting ammo, maybe we should close the gate. More coming."

"I need to get a better sense of the guardian's mobility," Curt said. "I've got an idea about how to fix that power problem. It'll take a lot of reconfiguration but... it'll solve it for good. Only I need to know..."

"It's got about half an hour mobility left in it," Keesha said.

"We only need five minutes. Send it after the stragglers..."

Keesha nodded. Did he really have a way to fix the power drain? "I'm going to put it on autonomous for a few minutes."

"I don't know, Keesha," Lyle2 said doubtfully.

But she'd already flicked the buttons, started the steel golem on its way. It rumbled toward the oncoming zombies, heading straight for a phalanx of the living dead, the nearest of them about twenty yards off.

"Lyle," Keesha said, her heart pounding, "get ready to close the gate fast if we have to..." There was no way to be sure the guardian wouldn't break down out there, with the gate wide open...

The guardian plowed into the closest group of zombies, moving on its own initiative in autonomous mode, its arms outstretched. A shabby male shambler tried to move past it—the robot's left arm swept out, pulled the walking corpse into its steely bear-hug—a cadaverous blue-skinned woman almost got past on the right but the guardian grabbed the braineater around the neck with a pincer, and simply snipped her head off.

"*Really* nice, Keesha," Curt said, grinning with excitement.

The guardian was bulldozing through zombies, spraying blood and

A particularly enterprising vulture swooped down and lit on the shoulder of a zombie in a highway patrolman's uniform.

ground-up zombie flesh in a pinwheel display of red flecked with bits of yellow bone.

One of the zombies in a tattered basketball player's uniform slipped past while the robot squeezed the others. Curt aimed carefully, with two hands on the gun, and fired—the zombie's head jerked and it fell to its knees, flopped onto its face.

"Ha! See, I can shoot if I take my time…"

Zombies moaned and were Osterized into red paste, blood fountaining like red wings to either side of the robot.

"Enough!" Curt declared. "But girl—that was *gorgeous!*"

Keesha looked at him. *Gorgeous?*

He went on excitedly, "All we need to do is rethink the power source! I've got something in mind I've wanted to try for a couple years now…Just switch that bad boy off in front of the gate and let's button it up. We'll hose your baby off later after the fence discourages the zombies…"

She hesitated, thinking that Curt was giving too many orders. Still, he made sense. She put the guardian back on remote control, brought it quickly to the front gate.

"Wait!" Curt yelled. "Cover me!" He ran out into the desert, and to the right, out of her line of sight.

"Curt! You stupid damn——"

But he was already coming back, pushing his motorcycle in a run. "Left it outside! We might need it!" Breathing hard, he pushed the Kawasaki through the gate and set up its kickstand.

There were still zombies staggering toward them, obliviously wading ankle deep through the freshly ground-up remains of their brain-eating colleagues. The reek of blended innards rolled through the gate—decayed blood and shit and some deliquescent essence of primal hatred. Keesha gagged and stepped back.

Holding her breath, she switched off the guardian, the machine facing outward, as Lyle2 pushed the gate shut, then ran for the switch box.

Moments later the electric fence was humming, and the sound and stench of zombies frying against the sparking metal began again; the sizzling and popping and burning road-kill smell that she'd grown so use to.

"IT'S ALL ABOUT THESE old bio-converters," Curt said, rubbing his hands briskly together. He and Keesha were standing in a wide wooden workshed, looking at a row of six biofuel converters, like misshapen steel urns lined up against the wall. "We'll need all six. Two to a guardian..."

Keesha shook her head firmly. "A complete redesign at this point... uh-uh. Not practical."

"It's not a complete redesign—we'll keep your blades, just move 'em a little. And we'll add the new power system."

"*No*, Curt. Because if it doesn't work I'll have to start over again. I'm going to find some way to get my guardians to the base."

"They can get there under their own power if you'll let me redesign them."

"Even if we had enough power they're too slow. Have to scrounge up a truck."

"So I'll help you find the truck but we still need to rethink the—"

"Curt?" Keesha interrupted, looking him in the eye. "It's not going to happen. You can build another one your way—on your own."

"That'll take too long—and you've probably used up most of the best CPU's and—"

"Curt? *No.*"

She looked at him—and a hardness came into his face.

He didn't have his pistol on him. But…

But then he smiled, the corners of his eyes crinkling. "It's your invention." He shrugged. "We'll talk about it later."

She didn't want to talk—she was tired and worried. The guardian worked—but didn't, all at once. She turned away, a little afraid to have her back to him. She wanted to trust him. But she didn't, not yet…all at once.

She went to the bunker, cleaned up, changed into her clean coveralls, decided to eat and rest and then work on guardian two.

Keesha had just finished something resembling beef stew when Curt came down the narrow concrete stairs, carrying a large bottle of clear fluid. His hair was wet, slicked back, his face and hands clean and he wore only cut-offs, and no shirt.

She stared at the label on the bottle. "Is that really vodka?"

"Sure as hell is. The real deal, scavenger's delight. Had it in my bike's saddlebag—I was gonna trade it to the owner of this place for some stuff. Did I see you've got some orange juice?"

She snorted. "Orange juice! We have some yellow powdered stuff they call orange flavoring."

"Close enough! Add water and vodka, stir, it's a cocktail. You've been feeding me so I'm sharing this with you. You game?"

"You need to ask?" She hadn't had a real drink in almost a year.

He ate one of the glutinous stews as she made the drinks in plastic cups. She noticed he was sitting on the edge of her cot, which was taking a pretty big liberty, but she said nothing about it. *Vodka. The real deal.*

They had a couple of drinks, then a couple more—the vodka made the ersatz orange juice taste almost good—and she told him about herself, about her parents and the guy she'd been hooked up with, at the base, all three killed on a food foray out of Base 23.

"Looking for food, becoming food," she said bitterly.

"You see them get killed?" Curt asked, matter-of-factly.

"No. Other people saw it. Not like I was real surprised it happened. Most people who go out to score food get killed out there, eventually. The only kinda safe place is the base itself and it's not all that safe."

"Who was the guy you were into?"

"Jared. Dad was some Jewish Greek guy, his mom was Mexican. He was…he just never panicked, never gave up. Just laughed at the zombies."

"Not laughing now," Curt muttered.

She thought that was a mean thing to say but she let it pass. "I saw my dad turn up…anyway, his body…as a zombie."

"You shoot him?"

"Sure. And buried him."

He nodded. It was kind of a tradition for the child to kill a zombied parent themselves if they could, lay the body to rest that way. Putting zombie relatives out of their misery almost had the status of a funeral now.

Keesha started crying as she finished the story. That was Curt's cue, and he took it. He put his arms around her, to comfort her, and she leaned in against him, looked up at him, and he took that cue too, and kissed her. She reached up to the wall switch, turned off the light. A little illumination came from the door, an indirect glow from the light at the top of the stairs. They kissed a while and then got undressed, and twined around one another on the cot.

He wasn't a great lover; he was kind of mechanical about it. When she looked into his eyes there was a clinical gleam in them, like an expression of scientific curiosity. But she reveled in the physical intimacy, the sheer bodily closeness; she exulted in the safety of an underground bunker, knowing Lyle2 was patrolling up above, and the electric fence was working. She was in a safe place in a man's arms, feeling him inside her…

Once when she opened her eyes, looking past Curt's shoulder, she saw the outline of another man standing in the doorway; a dark silhouette, watching them. She tensed—but then Lyle2 turned away, and went up the stairs.

LATER…AS THEY snuggled on the cot—Curt was pressed against her from behind, arms around her—he murmured, "I lost my folks, too. We were in a Tucson high rise and the braineaters got in…Me and my uncle escaped, the only ones to get out alive. A roamer killed my uncle, shot me, and left me for dead—for zombie food. But I crawled under a car, and waited, and someone came along, and I heard them talking. Living people! They were from the colony in the old prison… And they took me along, nursed me back to health. But I decided, after that, the world needed…needed *scouring*, you know? *Cleansing.* And what I've been wanting to do doesn't just stop a zombie, it *obliterates* them. It destroys the zombie virus in the process—destroys any microorganism in there. It's *real* purging."

That did sound good to her. And now she was willing to listen…

Especially when he kissed the back of her neck.

HIS ENTHUSIASM FOR THE redesign swept her along. And her own fervor grew over the next two weeks as they carefully cleaned off the first guardian, rebuilt its slaughter-system, and then scrounged in methodical madness through the piles of mechanical clutter; through jumbles of cybernetic hardware and electronic detritus, till they found what they needed. Lyle2 lifted the heavier parts and held them up as they were fitted.

They worked as long as there was daylight, and went to bed exhausted; Keesha slept on her cot in the bunker, Curt on a foam rubber slab in the shed. Mornings he'd come to her, and sometimes they'd make love. Mostly, he seemed obsessed with just getting the redesign done.

And they worked on, stopping only for bathroom breaks or to eat freeze-dried gunk, standing up in the workshed with tray and spoons in hand.

When they slept, Lyle2 patrolled the lot, or stood silently in the corner of the bunker, recharging.

On the evening of the fourteenth day, hands burning from corrosive chemicals and cuts, Keesha straightened up, her back crackling, and said, "I think Chuck's done." *Chuck* was the last of the three robots.

They'd named them because the resort to available parts gave each one a distinct appearance, almost a personality. The first one was Gordo, Spanish for fat, because he was the bulkiest; the second was Black Betty, because the robot's chassis and outer plates were singed black and there was a suggestion of something like a female bust in her outline; the third one, taller and more man-shaped, was Chuck Norris, after some actor Curt had seen on an old movie download.

Face smeared with grease and oil, Curt grinned at her. "They're beautiful, almost as pretty as you."

"Oh, some compliment, comparing these things to me…"

"Hey, you're their mom and I'm their dad. Proud parents! Let's get the remote, activate all units and get 'em out to the gate…"

Lyle2 surprised Keesha by speaking up, behind them. She hadn't known he was there. "You want to do a test *tonight?* It's getting late. After dark the zombies get kinda energetic and harder to see…"

Curt glanced at Lyle2, irritated. "Yeah, I want to do a test tonight. We've busted ass to get here. I want to know if was all wasted…"

Keesha nodded. "What the hell, let's do it." She'd grown used to letting Curt call the shots. Sometimes it bothered her, but mostly it was a relief.

She activated the three big robots, and sent them rolling hummingly out of the shed, Gordo in the lead and the others following. In the fading light they looked like mythical creatures of metal. She arrayed them just inside of the front gate.

There was something hissing right on the other side of gate…

"Open it," Curt told Lyle2.

Keesha thought she saw a look of irritation on Lyle2's artificial face, but the preservation bot unlocked the gate and slid it open.

A group of seven zombies immediately shambled in through the gate; most of them had been men. Curt activated the guardians and all three robots advanced on rumbling treads toward the braineaters. He set the guardians to *response* and they responded immediately, grabbing armfuls of zombies.

Chuck was the first to get his prey prepped. A bearded black zombie was quickly decapitated by Chuck's snipping left claw; the guardian dropped the spouting body and focused on the other zombie gripped writhing in the crook of its implacable, piston-powered right arm. Once a skinny Chicano teen with gang tattoos on his neck, Chuck's prize was now a growling, grunting, snapping braineater. There were no blades on the exterior of Chuck's steel chest—instead, two large metal flanges whirred open, exposing the four-foot-wide hopper Curt had taken from a harvesting robot.

Inside the hopper—within the robot's midsection—razor-sharp blades spun rapaciously; beneath the blades, enzyme sprays would separate from unusable parts and incineration waited to sterilize leftover zombie hash.

Chuck lifted the zombie up, turned it upside down, thrust the struggling living corpse headfirst down into the processor, jamming the Chicano zombie head and shoulders into its robotic interior. Keesha watched closely—and was relieved to see that the suction mechanism was effectively keeping blood from escaping as the zombie was ground up.

Merrily meat-grinding, the robot forced the living corpse between the mechanical jaws, cramming the zombie ever deeper: the head and shoulders had vanished into the hopper, the arms and chest were vanishing inch by inch; down and down the living corpse went, till the kicking legs were consumed...and finally the twitching feet.

Curt and Keesha waited breathlessly.

The robot hesitated, like a man at a feast who'd eaten too much—laboring servos keened...

"Come on—go to stage two goddammit, Chuck!" Curt said, grinding his teeth. "Burn it, convert it—*go!*"

Then a black-streaked water vapor geysered up from vents opening on the robot's back, whistling as it gushed—all the moisture of the ground-up corpse suddenly expelled. It was followed by dark brown smoke, odorous of diesel and cooked meat. The exhaust curled thickly over them in a putrid cloud...

"Yes!" Curt crowed, eyes sparkling in delight as he looked at the green light on the remote. "Fully powered! A robot has been powered up *from eating zombie flesh!* That, my Keesha—*that* is biofuel!"

She nodded, feeling a rush at their achievement as she watched the robots harvesting zombies.

All the guardians were crushing zombies to them; they used their sharp grippers to decapitate one, strip the other of clothes before feeding the living dead-man into biofuel conversion hoppers.

A female braineater in a glittery G-string—a flailing zombie who'd once been a stripper—stumbled past the occupied guardians. The almost nude zombie had lost all flesh on its face—nothing remained but eyes in a skull. She had long luxurious blonde hair and two pendulous breasts tipped with sparkly pasties. A silicon implant glinted from a crooked oozing slash in her right breast. Curt drew the pistol jammed in his waistband, and quite deliberately shot the stripper zombie through the knees, firing twice. The skull-faced zombie fell flat—but kept crawling toward him, pulling itself with clawed fingers.

Curt flicked the controls of the remote in his other hand so that Black Betty turned toward the stripper. Using rotational wrist articulation to switch its end effectors from pincers to barbed steel talons, Black Betty ducked down—middle chassis sliding down on her leg columns—and scooped the stripper zombie up. She fed the shrieking braineater feet-first into the hopper. The blonde tresses went in last, and for a moment the internal grinder was jammed by hair…then it freed itself and filthy vapor gouted from Black Betty's vents…

Green lights flashed on the remote. *Charged.*

"Well," Curt said, chuckling, "These babies work *beautifully.*" He seemed deeply moved. Keesha thought he might start weeping with emotion—but Curt only bit his lip and finished in a hoarse whisper, "They're just…gorgeous."

Lyle2 closed the gate before more zombies could lurch into the yard…

But before he could lock it, the gate rolled back, opening on its own. Keesha stared. "What the fuck! You fixed the gate motor, Lyle?"

Lyle2 shook his head. "Not me. I didn't know it had one…"

"Must've been that guy out there," Curt said. "He's got some kinda gate remote." He pointed to a large box-truck on the dusty road leading to the robot graveyard. It was about thirty yards out, rumbling toward the gate, trailing a rooster tail of dust. They stared, wondering which way to jump, as the box truck slowed at the gate, drove ponderously through, then pulled up in the loading area, engine chugging in idle. A stocky man in greasy mechanic's coveralls and Kevlar vest climbed out, a submachine gun in his right hand. He was a short, thick-bodied man with a wrinkled bald head, eyes hidden in sunglasses. He ogled the guardians and turned to Curt, "What the fuck isth going on here?" He had a deep voice but a lisp—most of his teeth were missing, the stumps ragged. Looked like he'd lost them recently in a fight.

"And who'd you be?" Curt asked, drawing his pistol from his waist band.

"My name's Joe Purvith…" He licked his lips and pronounced the name more carefully. "*Purvis*…and I'm the *owner* of thith fucking facility! Who the Jeebus fuck you *think?*" He pointed the submachine gun at Curt. "I figure I know who you are—you're the guy ripping off my stuff!"

Curt laughed. "The owner of this *facility?* Your abandoned junk heap!"

"I left my brother to watch it for me—where is he?"

"We cleared out the zombies for you," Lyle2 said. "Your brother was probably one of them. He must've screwed up and let the braineaters in. As for ownership—that's not really an applicable concept anymore, dude."

Purvis gaped at Lyle2. "And you! You're my goddamn prethervation bot! What the hell you people done to it!"

"There're zombies following him in," Lyle2 noted, looking past Purvis. "About forty yards out and closing."

"Look, we're gonna leave here soon, Mr. Purvis," Keesha said. "We cleaned up your zombies for you and we'll deal with those out there, so—"

"And you've been eating my food, like as not—and *what the hell are those things!*" Purvis pointed at Gordo.

"I can show you what they are, Joe," Curt said.

Shivering at something in Curt's voice, Keesha looked at him. "*Curt?*"

Purvis snarled, "You drop that pithtol of yours and then we'll figure out what I'm gonna do with you! All of you, toth your gun down!"

"Sure, I'll 'toth' it," Curt said, dropping his gun casually aside as he strolled two steps over to Keesha.

"Curt—no."

He smiled at her, held her eyes with his—and grabbed the remote from her, flicked its controller…

Gordo stiffened into life, then rolled down on Purvis who swung the gun toward the robot and fired. Bullets struck sparks from Gordo's steel body and then the guardian grabbed Purvis—who squeezed the trigger spasmodically, his bullets thunk-thunking into the ground, as the hulking robot clutched him to it. Gordo used one pincer to adroitly strip the survivalist's clothes and Kevlar vest off, peeling him like fruit; then it stuffed him, shrieking, headfirst into its hopper, grinding him up inside its chest, suction keeping most of the blood from spraying out. Purvis's warbling scream suddenly cut off and there was only the gurgling growl of the grinders…

"Oh God, Curt…" Keesha shook her head and looked at Lyle2, who gave her a fairly realistic look of mild disgust in return.

"Hey," Curt said, shrugging, "The guy was going to kill us! You *know* he was!"

"Good possibility of it," Lyle2 admitted.

"You don't know that for sure!" Keesha shouted. "We might have worked things out with him!"

"Couldn't take the chance," Curt insisted mildly, shrugging broadly. "I mean come on—you never shot a roamer?"

"Once," she said reluctantly. "Tried to rape me."

"'Purvith' was no better. He was going to kill you. And now we know a guardian works with human flesh just as well—fresh, *living* human flesh can power these babies too! It took the charge! Biofuel is biofuel!"

"Here comes more biofuel," Lyle2 said dourly, pointing out the gate.

"Let Gordo handle the first of them…"

And Gordo did; Black Betty and Chuck got the other zombies, with what seemed to Keesha like an almost human alacrity.

"What happens when they run out of room inside themselves?" Lyle2 asked, as the last of the zombies, a shoeless, noseless man in a business suit, was ground up in Chuck.

"Of course, a lot of human body mass is water, which is boiled off and vented by the mechanism," Curt said, rubbing his hands together gleefully as he watched Gordo. "The useful parts are converted to electrical energy. There's still some crude waste matter left over. Ah, and here it comes."

A flange flipped open on Gordo's lower rear and a thin stream of gray powder jetted out; it became a sudden dump of ashes and clunking bits piled up on the ground.

"Didn't do a perfect job of strippin' 'em," Curt observed, poking through the pile with the toe of his shoe. "That wristwatch—wonder if it's still ticking…"

3.

PURVIS'S ROOMY BOX TRUCK came in handy for the planned trip to Base 23. The survivalist had loaded the truck with scrap robot parts from around the southwest. Most of those Curt dumped in the scrapyard to make room for the guardians. The back of the box truck was just roomy enough for the three big robots. The truck engine was biofueled, supplemented by solar power—Curt worked feverishly for five days, customizing its drive system.

On the sixth morning after Purvis made his contribution to Gordo's energy charge, they directed the big robots out into the desert, following them in the truck. Keesha was riding shotgun in the truck's cab, controlling the robots from there; Curt was driving, Lyle2 crammed between them. Gordo, Black Betty and Chuck trundled ahead of them toward the small crowd of shamblers…

Keesha glanced at Curt, thinking he seemed a different man now. He wasn't quite the man who'd made love to her over the past few weeks. They'd been close, for a while—anyway, *she'd* felt close. She'd felt bonded with him. Now it was as if he'd been replaced by someone else, almost the way Lyle had been replaced by Lyle2. The big difference was, she trusted Lyle2. The killing of Purvis had shaken her trust in Curt.

But likely Curt was right—Purvis had to die. He probably wouldn't have come around. Still…

"There they are," Curt said, suddenly. "Robot lunch."

There were only about eleven zombies currently wandering in a stumbling herd between the robot graveyard and the open desert. The ranks of the living dead were getting thinner, out here. They tended to crowd around the cities and highways.

Curt pulled up the truck and they watched as the guardians decapitated six zombies, then methodically converted five others to energy. "Like chain-sawing tree limbs and tossing them on a campfire," Curt said.

Tree limbs don't bleed, Keesha thought. But she wasn't going to say it out loud. If you thought zombies were still people, you were a fool.

Curt looked musingly at the sprawled, reeking decapitated bodies.

Fully charged, the robots had no use for the excess corpses, at the moment. "It's a shame to waste the biofuel," Curt said. "We could direct a guardian to stuff 'em in the back of the truck for later if we run short of fuel…"

"Ugh," Keesha said.

"I second that ugh," said Lyle2. "Big time unpleasant to have rotting corpses in the back of the truck."

Curt glanced at Lyle2 in irritation. "You going to pretend you're human enough to be repelled by that?"

Lyle2 looked calmly back at him. "I second anything Keesha says, or does."

Curt shrugged and scanned at the horizon. "Looks like the coast's clear for the moment." He pressed a button on the dashboard. The back of the truck lowered down to become a ramp. "So, robot boy—you got a program for riding a motorcycle?"

Lyle frowned, and seemed to think, searching his memory storage. "Yes. I do."

"Then take my bike out of the back, ride ahead a little, scout the way. Use all your sensors, top power. See any roamers or zombies or ravines, any problems, you let us know."

Lyle2 glanced at Keesha. She nodded. The preservation bot said, "Okay. How about fuel for the bike?"

Curt hooked a thumb at the truck's rear. "It's fueled up. There's more in cans in the back of the truck. Let us know when you need it. When you need a charge, Black Betty's set up to feed you the juice. It'll be real romantic."

Lyle2 stared at him a long moment—then he shrugged and looked at Keesha.

She got out of his way and he climbed out of the truck. After a minute they heard the sound of the motorcycle.

Wearing the black helmet, shotgun strapped across his back, Lyle2 rode to the front of the truck where he sat straddling the idling bike as Keesha directed Gordo, Chuck and Black Betty into temporary storage. They rolled up the ramp, into the back of the truck, wedged themselves against the supplies piled behind the cab.

"Let's go," Curt said. "We've got a long haul ahead of us."

He's really taken over, Keesha thought. But right now all she cared about was getting back to Base 23. If Curt started screwing up, she'd take control back from him. Whether he liked it or not.

Lyle2 waved, gunned the Kawasaki and rode on ahead, along the old gravel fire road winding through the desert, and the truck lurched into motion to follow.

"How far, you think, to the base?" Curt asked, as he rolled the window up against the dust.

"About a hundred forty miles."

Keesha felt a growing excitement at the prospect of getting home—what had passed for home, for some years. She had a chance to really protect the base with the new robots.

The sun behind them, they rumbled and bumped along the sketchy track between low hillocks, heading southwest, toward Base 23. She watched nervously for Lyle2, saw him from time to time up ahead, weaving between saguaros and rugged sandstone boulders.

They drove for an hour, seeing no zombies and few living things—the occasional darting lizard, a few vultures against the aluminum-colored sky, and once Keesha glimpsed a roadrunner.

Every time she looked at Curt he was smiling, focused, leaning eagerly forward to peer through the dusty windshield. Sometimes his happy smile became a strained, almost involuntary grin.

She shook her head. "Curt—I don't know when I last saw anyone so... *happy*. Just don't see it much anymore. It's starting to spook me, man."

Curt chuckled. "Wasn't much to be happy about, mostly, till now. But now—just think about it! We have a chance to transform this planet, Keesha. The trick is to develop *self-replicating* zombie-fueled robots. They build more of themselves, with the same programming imperative to destroy and consume zombies. They'll scour the world! And, you know, when people get in the way of that—they can go in the hopper too, just like Purvis."

Keesha stared at him. "Curt, what the fuck?"

He hunched forward, knuckles white on the steering wheel. "Look—how many times have you seen roamers and raiders shot down by your pals at the base? Did you bitch about that?"

"That's self-defense, Curt."

"This is too. Best defense is a good offense." He glanced at her, his eyes hot and icy at once. "Hey—if you and me are going to be *together*, we got to be together on *everything*. Now listen—almost everyone's in our way, Keesha. I mean—what *are* most people? I figure they're in two categories, you know? People are mostly either zombies or robots."

"Zombies aren't the issue—"

"No, you don't get it. I mean people who haven't got the zombie virus, so-called regular healthy people. They are just zombies of another kind. All human beings are out there looking to eat your fucking brains in one way or another. They want to *use* you, Keesha…to just suck up your energy and consume you! And they're *all* dead inside! Trust me!" He was talking faster and faster, spittle from his mouth striking the steering wheel. His head trembled; veins stood out on his straining neck. "And there's the people who are like machines, never get past their little life programs! Like the ones who shot my uncle and left me to the tender mercies of the zombies in the street. Robots! Zombies and robots! The walking dead we feed our steel babies, girl, they're just the final stage of what human beings are anyway! If they're not zombies—

they're robots. So we make robots to kill zombies and to kill people like robots and people like zombies…"

Uh-oh, Keesha thought. *This is not good.*

"Do you *understand* what I mean, Keesha?" His teeth were clenched as he said it, his voice shriller as he spat out, "Or…*not?*"

"Um—yeah. I guess I do." *Keep him occupied. Because the guy is out of his fucking gourd.* "Yeah, Curt. I kind of gave up on people the first time I saw a guy kill another guy for a can of refried beans."

Say anything. It's all there in his voice. He's threatening you without saying it right out. Make a plan, Keesha.

Okay. She could get him to stop the truck, claim she needed to pee, then wait for her chance, knock Curt out. Take the truck and leave, head for Base 23.

"Keesha?"

She glanced at Curt. He was stealing looks at her. Frowning.

"Better keep your eyes on what passes for a road, Curt," she said, pointing.

He veered, the truck fishtailing, to avoid hitting a looming outcropping of sandstone. "Yeah. But Keesha? I said something really important, a minute ago. About trust. About you and me being together on everything. See there's a third category of people. Me and the people I'm with. Those people are going to be just fine. But that might not be very many people. So—are you one of those people…or not? You're either on the bus or off it."

Use your Broadway, Keesha.

"Yeah, duh, of *course*, you think I give up my pussy to every skinny white motherfucker comes along? You got the chops, the moves!" She tapped her forehead. "Right up here. That's what I'm looking for. Somebody smarter than me." She shrugged, hoping he bought into the flattery. No way she thought he was actually smarter than her.

The zombies in its grip squealed and gnashed helplessly.

He licked his lips and looked at her, then back at the road. Then back at her…

"The road, Curt…"

He looked up ahead, had to swerve again. "Sorry." He let out a long breath. "So you're on the bus. You're *okay*. That's cool, then. You and me, girl. You and me."

She changed the subject to robotics. "How'd you make a guardian self-replicating?"

They had a half hour of that and then she thought: *That's long enough. Do it now.*

"Curt? Can you stop this thing? I need to pee."

"What? Yeah, sure. Me too, in fact."

He honked, once, to let Lyle2 know they were stopping, and pulled up between two large outcroppings of rock. They looked around for zombies, saw none; saw nothing move at all. But when they got out they took their guns, of course. She had her assault rifle, he had Purvis's SMG.

She went behind a rock, tried to pee, finding it difficult when she thought about what she was going to have to do, after. She managed a little, got it over with quick. She stood up quickly, tugging her pants closed, and saw Curt peeing against a rock about ten yards away, his back to her.

This was her chance. Curt was flat-out crazy and he had control of the guardians. He might threaten the base. She had no intention of risking anyone at Base 23.

No need to bother Lyle2—who was just then riding back to them. She could just shoot Curt Curson down. Here and now. Shoot Curt in the back of the head, an easy shot from here—better to do it that way. She didn't want to leave him out here alive to be turned zombie. She owed him that anyway.

He was just finishing his pee, doing that dick-shaking thing men do.

She raised the rifle…took aim at the back of his head…

But…

She remembered him in the bunker; Curt twined with her on the cot. There had been moments of childlike tenderness, of real human need, in Curt…

Other times, he'd been like one of the robot people he talked about.

Maybe that was his problem. A particularly nasty case of the PTSD she'd seen in so many people. Hell, in most people.

Curt was stuck in who he was. He was trapped. He was a victim like everyone else dealing with the world falling down around them. How could she just abandon him? What if…

What if she could get through to him? Maybe she could get him to see that there were a lot of people worth saving.

Curt was zipping up his pants as Lyle2 circled up to them on the bike.

Curt hadn't hurt her, not yet. And she needed him to help her build more zombie-eating robots. Didn't she? Maybe not. Still—he was just a scared kid, inside, like everyone else. He couldn't mean everything he'd said…

She lowered the rifle—and he turned around, stretching. "I'd better check the truck fuel…"

"Sure."

He looked closely at her, his head cocked. "You okay? You seem kinda…"

"I'm okay. Just nervous. Exposed like this."

"I've got you guys covered," Lyle2 said, the shotgun in his hands.

Curt nodded and went to the truck. Lyle2 had opened his helmet, was looking around, the shotgun in his hands. But he kept looking over at her.

It seemed to Keesha that Lyle2 was watching her closely, too. He'd seen her point that gun at Curt. He knew something was wrong.

Curt walked to the truck and Lyle2 caught her eye, raised his eyebrows, then ducked his head toward Curt. He tapped the shotgun's breach.

You want me to…?

She hesitated—then shook her head.

Curt returned from the truck's cab. "Thing eats through fuel fast. Don't want to use the spare stuff unless we have to. Keep your eyes open." He turned to Lyle2. "You see anything out there? People, robots, zombies, anything?"

Lyle2 shook his head. "Couple of lizards."

"All right. We on the right track for the base?"

Lyle2 nodded. "My mapping says we're on the best possible route. Not like the crow flies but we're making good progress. I'll let you know if we get lost."

"You need to charge up?"

"Not yet. Need fuel for the bike though."

They refueled the bike from one of the cans in the back of the truck, then Curt said, "Let's move out." Calling out to Lyle2 as he rode off, "Watch for robot dinner along the way!"

"You want me to drive?" Keesha asked as they walked back to the truck cab.

"Nah."

Nah. He wasn't going to give up control for a moment, not of anything.

They climbed in, he slammed the driver's door shut with one hand, reaching for the ignition keys with the other. The truck roared, lurched off along the rutted road. The gravel had long since thinned to dirt and sand.

After a while she said, casually as she could, "Curt? You need to understand something about Base 23."

"Yeah? What's that?"

"You *can* trust people there. I'm not good buddies with all of them but we all watch each other's back. That's what matters. I've got two cousins there and a couple of real friends. You've gotta give them a chance."

Curt said nothing for a while. At last, his voice tightly controlled, he said, "What makes you think I'm not going to give anyone a chance?"

"The way you were talking before. Listen—I'm on your side, Curt. I am. I'm with you. But you don't want to throw away a good resource. These people save each other's lives every day. We need that. Give them a chance. Okay?"

He chewed his lower lip. Glanced at her. Looked back at the road. "Sure. If they're cool with me—I'll be cool with them."

Doing a mechanical bump and grind, the truck worked its way across the desert in a perpetual plume of dust, and the day wore on as the miles wore away.

IT WAS LATE AFTERNOON when they came to a highway, angling to the south. "Goes our way," Keesha said, "But there'll be zombies."

Curt gave his wolfish grin. "Truck's hungry." He turned south along the highway, signaling Lyle2 to parallel them on the other lane.

Within ten minutes they came to a cluster of shamblers limping across the road. The noise of their approach made the zombies turn gaping toward them. They were a dozen ragged, gaping, sunburnt figures with milky eyes; all of them had once been male. As they got closer she saw most of them were in the rags of Army uniforms.

Curt reached under the dashboard for the little toggle he'd installed. "What was the ideal speed we'd decided on for this, Keesha?"

"Twenty-five at most."

He nodded, slowed the truck to twenty-five. Now the zombies were trotting, stumbling, crawling toward the oncoming truck in a group. Too stupid to get out of the way.

Curt slowed the truck some more. "Thirty...twenty-eight...twenty-five miles per. And—here we go."

They plowed into the zombies, busting one up pretty good—blackened blood, bits of teeth splashed up onto the windshield. Seven or eight zombies were knocked down, a few to the side; at least four dragged bumpingly under the truck. The scooper reacted to the pressure, scraping the shrieking braineaters off the pavement; it jammed them up into the garbage-disposal-style blades under the truck's engine.

Keesha could feel the vibrations rise sickeningly up her spine as the rotors crunched zombie flesh, and spinning steel brushes turned by the front wheel axles propelled the shattered semihuman remains up into the box truck's biofuel processors...

As the vibration stopped they left the other shattered zombies behind, and picked up speed. Curt looked at the fuel gauge. "There it is—fully powered! The truck eats and digests, just like that! Worked *beautifully!*"

Humming to himself, Curt pressed the button for the washer to squirt soapy water onto the windshield, used the wipers to clean blood and a tooth and dust away.

But the stench of ground-up living dead rose with the persistence of a traumatic memory, wafting thickly through the cab so that Keesha gagged, retched, and rolled down the window to get some fresh air...

They continued down the highway. And the miles shambled by.

• • •

4.

NEAR DUSK, THE SKY going the dark blue of gunmetal, Curt was still straining at the steering wheel, eyes narrowed, breathing hard. Now and then he murmured something to himself. Keesha couldn't hear what he was saying over the growling engine.

They tooled around a long curve—and two more zombies loomed up, blocking the road: a gawping one-eyed woman in a stained wedding dress, a hollow-eyed man in a groom's suit.

"Romantic," Curt said. "Now for their honeymoon."

Keesha winced at that.

Curt slowed to twenty-five, ran the braineaters bumpingly over, ground them up, accelerated—and moved on.

In the side view Keesha glimpsed a bloodstained wedding veil, drifting away on the wind.

Another five miles, and Keesha spotted zombies shambling off-road to the west, walking between outcroppings of red sandstone, looking for their place in the food chain.

Keesha didn't mention them—she didn't want Curt off-roading now. She was eager to get to Base 23.

Ten minutes later they saw Lyle2 stopped on the road up ahead.

"What's he waving at us about?" Curt muttered.

The preservation bot was astride the idling Kawasaki, in the middle of the highway, pointing to a narrow asphalt side road.

"That's the turnoff for Base 23!" Keesha said, relief and excitement mingling in her.

Curt slowed, and they swung off the freeway, onto the side road.

"Just a few more miles," Keesha said. "And then I get to see if my friends are alive. And my cousins! There's better food there too, Curt. We've gotten good at hunting. Jackrabbit stew with sage…"

"Doesn't really matter to me. I've gotten used to eating any goddamn thing. Things get bad—I figure we can reprocess zombie flesh."

She looked at him. "Now you *are* fucking with me."

"Not a joke, girl. It can be done. Theory is, you turn 'em into a kind of mush for meat patties. You cauterize the stuff every which way—kill every micro-organism in it, add salt and pepper. Presto, instant protein..."

"Curt—that's still cannibalism."

"Like I fucking care. You're telling me you never ate any—Wait, what's that?"

Not far ahead, a six-foot-high metal gate blocked the way, linking two long stretches of barbed wire fence. Behind the gate two crude hulking bunkers flanked the road. They were a mix of sod and clay over scrounged metal debris. Machine gun barrels gleamed in the firing slots.

"That's the outer perimeter of Base 23!" Keesha said. "We're there!"

She looked at the side mirror, saw Lyle2 on the motorcycle riding behind them. He must've seen her reflection in the mirror—he raised a thumb's-up.

"Wait—look over there," Curt said, slowing the truck. "North."

She saw it then, as he brought the truck to a stop a few paces from the gate—a big section of fence had been torn down, forty yards to the right of the gate. There were a couple of sagging bodies hung awkwardly in the broken wire. Crows perched on the bodies, pecking busily at shattered skulls.

Keesha stared, feeling a sick chill. "That's not...encouraging."

"Better get the robots out," Curt said, his voice a growl.

He cut the engine and they climbed out, weapons in hand.

Lyle2 pulled up beside them, a ghostly following of dust continuing past him as he braked the Kawasaki. He shut off the bike and came to stand near Keesha, watching the back of the truck lower, the robots roll creakingly out.

Curt said, "I think I'm gonna go to *autonomous* pretty soon on this, so I can be free to use the SMG. If I need to."

"You're gonna set them on autonomous?" Lyle2 said, shaking his head with a disdain that seemed very Lyle. "They could attack *us.* They'll go for anything nearby!"

"Not if we're a proper distance back and they're working on zombies," Curt said. "If they come at us I can always switch 'em back on manual. I'll give you both plenty of warning before autonomous mode..."

As Black Betty rolled by her, Keesha looked at the blood-spattered treads. Clipping off heads, Keesha concluded, wasn't terribly hygienic. They'd have to work on that. She didn't like being this close to zombie blood.

The hulking guardian robots did a wide turn, to rumble past the truck toward the gate. When they'd gotten by the truck's cab, Curt flicked the controls, and they lined up side by side facing the bunkers.

His fingers flicked again and they began rolling slowly, implacably toward the gate. Curt walked behind them with the remote control, followed by Keesha and Lyle2. But Lyle2 was walking backwards, watching their six, scanning for zombies.

Keesha was telling herself that the break in the fence wasn't as dangerous as it looked. There was still the inner perimeter, holding the line. Her cousins, and her friends, could still be alive.

"You see anything out there?" she asked Lyle2.

"Buncha zombies, maybe from the Indian Rez, but not close. But not that far away either. Looks like they might be feasting on something. Or someone. Likely to be other braineaters already inside the fence."

Far ahead, down the road past the gate, she could just make out the inner fence and the sheet-metal buildings of Base 23. There was the top of the old hangar they'd converted into central housing; there was the wooden watchtower, too far away to tell if anyone was in it.

"Stop the robots right there, Curt," she said firmly. "Or we're gonna freak out the guards."

Gordo, Chuck and Black Betty creaked to a stop and she hurried past them, rifle ready in her hands. "Curt, Lyle—wait here, I gotta let 'em know it's me or we'll all get shot." A few paces more and she shouted, "Yo, hello the gate! It's Keesha! Who's there? Burke? That you?"

No answer from the bunkers. The machine gun muzzles didn't twitch—and now she could see they were tilted at useless angles, down and to the side. Another bad sign.

"I'm coming through the gate!" she yelled. "Hold your fire!" She trotted up to the gate, fishing the gate key from her pocket. She used the key to unlock the padlock, and pushed the gates open. "Hey! Anybody in the bunkers?"

No response. Licking her lips, blinking in the declining sun, Keesha raised the assault rifle and went through the gate, up to the back of the bunker on her right. The cloud of flies told her what she'd find before she looked into the open door. There was old Burke, who was usually watching the gate, sitting up under a gun, back to the firing slit. He was facing the door, his head blown raggedly off above the eyebrows. In his right hand was the shotgun he'd used; in his left was an empty bottle of whiskey.

There were two corpses on the floor, sprawled face down at Burke's feet. Bluebottle flies buzzed angrily over their shattered heads.

The story was there to see. The zombies had gotten through the break in the fence, in the dark; they'd come at Burke from behind. He'd turned and shot them but he didn't get them all, not in time. Not before one had bitten him—she could see the chunk of flesh missing from his ankle. He'd killed himself before he could turn zombie.

He'd been her friend—almost an uncle to her.

She felt numb, turning away from him. *Go with numb. It always works.* There was no time to grieve now.

Keesha found no one at all in the other bunker. Just dried blood crusted on the floor.

She turned away from the bunkers at the sound of engines coming from the base. She squinted against the sun, shaded her eyes with a hand, and made out a big vehicle coming their way, raising dust.

The Kill Bus was coming.

Keesha smiled, heartened, her pulse racing. "They're alive, Lyle!" she shouted. "Must've seen us from the watchtower!" After a moment she added, to herself, "Some of 'em are alive, anyway."

She turned to see Lyle2 walking toward her, smiling faintly. "We lose the gate sentry?"

"Yeah. Burke. Maybe some others, too."

"You're going to have to explain me to them."

Keesha shrugged. "So what. They'll have to get used to it."

She turned, frowning, at the rumbling of the guardians coming through the gate.

"Curt? Keep them back, my people don't know if those damn robots are friendly! They might…"

"They're gonna learn they're unfriendly if they don't treat 'em with respect," Curt said, coming through the gate behind the trundling bots, submachine gun strapped over his left shoulder, the remote control in his hands.

Gordo's bucketlike head swiveled; its camera eye scanned for enemies…

Black Betty's grippers were opening, closing; opening, closing…

Chuck's grippers had gone to slice mode; his hopper was open, blades whirring inside it…

"Curt—just hold them back, they look like they're ready to attack, goddammit!"

Curt glanced at her, scowling, eyes narrowed. But he stopped the robots just inside the gate.

The Kill Bus was driving up—it was an old olive-green troop transport bus, with the upper half cut away, everything above the windshield missing. Two men stood at gun scrap-metal emplacements behind the driver—Keesha recognized red-headed McCrae, and the dirty, bushy-bearded face of Benzicker, both men wearing dusty goggles.

The driver was Alvarez, an aging Mexican with a corona of white hair, his expression worried. But it always was.

The Kill Bus swerved around, turning horizontal to them, and stopped about twenty-five yards away. Keesha counted seven men and two women standing up in back, crowded on the near side, all of them with guns in their hands except for Daisy, the Apache woman with her hunter's crossbow cadged from a hardware store. Her father, Barking Dog, stood near her, a double-barreled shotgun pointed toward Curt and the guardians. None of them looked glad to see her.

Keesha shook her head, mystified. "Why the fuck you got those weapons pointed at us, McCrae? You can see it's me. And you can see I'm still alive. And I've brought the guardians!"

"We let some outsiders in when you were gone," McCrae said, his voice gravelly. He was looking at Curt as he spoke. "One of 'em broke the rules, left the base without permission. Tried to scavenge for booze somewhere. Stole a truck to do it. He was supposed to be standing guard on the bunker there. Zombies swarmed him, he came back drunk, panicking, rode through the fence, busted a whole in the inner perimeter… Zombies flooded right in after him."

Keesha groaned. "What an asshole. Where's he now?"

"I shot him myself. But not before we got swarmed by zombies.

We're still cleaning 'em up. We lost seventeen people, Keesha. Haven't had a chance to bury poor Burke. So we made a new rule—*No Outsiders*. We meet 'em outside and *if* we decide they're okay, then maybe. But if they come to the base without asking—we shoot 'em." He looked at Lyle2. "And what the hell is that? That's not your brother."

Keesha nodded, opened her mouth to explain Lyle2 and Curt—she never got it out.

Curt shouted, "*Fuck you!* The whole bunch of you! I can see what you are. You're fuel! I knew it'd fucking come to this…"

Keesha turned to him, her hands up warningly. "Curt—don't do anything! Stand down for Chrissakes!"

"They said they're gonna shoot me!"

"Not when I—*No!*"

The robots were rolling forward, arms outstretched, whirring, heads turning, looking for targets, moving toward the bus, fast as they were capable.

Curt shouted, "Get back, Keesha! They're going autonomous!"

"No—goddammit Curt! Give me the controller!"

Keesha sprinted toward Curt—as gunfire erupted from the Kill Bus, ricochets ringing from the massive robots.

Bad move, she thought, shooting at those things. They were programmed to protect against all attackers, not just zombies. "Don't fire at the robots!" she shouted, but her words were cut up by the cracks of gunfire. The bus engine was whining as Alvarez tried to restart it.

Gunfire from the Kill Bus whined over her head and thumped into the bunker where Curt was stepping into cover, ignoring the flies and the dead.

"Keesha—get down!" Lyle2 yelled, running toward her.

Bullets strafed up the asphalt, probably intended for Curt—but striking Lyle, knocking him down. He wasn't armored like the guardians.

She lunged through the door of the bunker, and fell, dropping her rifle—tripped by Curt—her face an inch from the rotting flesh of a zombie. "Fuck!"

Retching, she got to her feet—turned to see Curt just inside the door, pointing the submachine gun at her. "Are you with me or not?"

"I..." Keesha hesitated, feeling like she wasn't going to make him believe her—and then the screams started outside.

She looked out the door—saw the robots tearing into the Kill Bus. Black Betty was smashing through the engine with one steel gripper, flames licking up as the other gripper rammed through the windshield, grippers decapitating Alvarez. Guns fired to no effect as Black Betty gutted McCrae and Benzicker. Chuck and Gordo crunched into the body of the bus, the metal ripping with a *squeeeee* sound so the bus seemed to scream. Bullets sparked off the guardians as they plucked men and women from their posts, snipped off this one's head, thrust that one into the hopper. Keesha saw Daisy disappear headfirst, screaming, into Gordo's steel belly; Daisy's father, Barking Dog, tried to pull the robot's grippers from her—Barking Dog's head seemed to pop from his body like the flicked cap from a shaken beer bottle. Keesha saw the gleam of the gripper shearing through his neck.

"Oh God, Curt. What have you done...?"

She turned to see a wolfish grin of delight on Curt's face as he backed out the door of the bunker—and then she knew. "You *wanted* this! All along you wanted this! You'd have killed them no matter what! You forced a fight the first chance you got! You *prick!*"

The grin became a quivering grimace. "You're not *with* me, Keesha. Are you."

He pointed the SMG at her head—and then Curt's feet went out from under him and he fell backwards, dropping the controller.

Lyle2 had hold of Curt's ankle, was pulling him out of the bunker

Curt's feet went out from under him and he fell backwards,
dropping the controller.

onto the road. Lyle2 was on one knee—his right leg was shattered by bullets, pistons, circuits and wires exposed and dangling.

Keesha looked around for her rifle. The glare of the setting sun outside made the interior of the bunker dark.

"Stay away from my sister!" Lyle2 yelled.

"She's not your sister, you can't have a sister, you're a fucking robot!" Curt yelled.

Keesha looked through the door again, saw Curt kick the preservation bot in the face, hard, so that Lyle2 lost his grip on him. Curt got to his feet, fumbling with his submachine gun.

Beyond them, Chuck was tearing McCrae apart, stuffing him a piece at a time into his hopper.

Keesha found her rifle, snatched it up, rushed outside—and stopped.

Curt was there, to one side of the door, pressing his submachine gun to her left temple with one hand. The controller was in his other hand. "Drop it or I'll blow your brains out. *Now*, Keesha."

She let the rifle clatter to the ground. "Curt...just take the bots and go."

He shook his head. "No. There are *more* of those people on this base. They're *all* robots or zombies, Keesha. The only robots I tolerate work for me. And you—you act like a robot is your brother! You're halfway inhuman, inside, Keesha. You're not on my side. I should kill you right now. It's funny—not as easy as I thought it'd be..."

Lyle2 was getting up, balancing awkwardly on his intact foot. One of his artificial eyes had been shot away, its socket smoking.

Curt stepped back from her and turned to fire a short burst at Lyle2—who went down once more, arms jerking spasmodically, smoke and sparks spitting from holes in his chest.

Curt grinned when she turned to go for her gun, pointed the SMG at her. "Don't do it. Kick the rifle away. Maybe I'll let you live. Maybe."

Keesha licked her lips. Her heart was thumping almost loud enough to drown out a final pealing shriek from a woman on the bus…

She looked at the rifle at her feet—and kicked it away.

"You know," Curt said, "I really can't trust you. That makes it crystal clear. That makes up my mind for me." He thumbed the controls on the controller. Gordo turned away from the bus—where the other two robots continued their feasting—and rumbled toward Keesha and Curt and Lyle2.

"Kee…" Lyle2 said, lying on the ground, his voice distorted. "…sha…"

Gordo rolled up to within a few yards of Keesha, its arms extended.

"Consumed by your own offspring," Curt said. "That's your destiny, girl. That's what happens eventually."

Gordo loomed over her—she turned to run and it swiped at her. The blow was like a baseball bat smacking her on the back.

Stunned, she was thrown skidding on her face, the world gyrating around her. Grinding her teeth at the pain, she turned onto her back—looked up at Gordo looming over her—

Lyle2 shot up from the ground like a taut spring uncoiling, his single intact leg propelling him at Curt. He knocked Curt back, grappling, wrestling for the SMG. He turned the gun toward Curt and the weapon spurted fire. Curt staggered backwards. He fell against the bunker, gasping hoarsely, sliding down to sit on the asphalt, welling bullet holes punched in his chest, teeth bared in pain. Blood gushed onto his lap.

Keesha was scrambling back from Gordo. It was close, almost close enough.

Lyle2 dropped the submachine gun, and scooped up the controller. "I…can't operate it. Too much blood on it…I'm too damaged…"

The guardian had backed her up against the barbed wire fence. It was lowering its midsection, so its arms could grab Keesha—and Lyle2 lurched toward it, hopping quickly to get between her and her creation. He dropped the controller as he came, his grip failing.

"Lyle—don't get near it!" she shouted.

Lyle2 turned to face Keesha as Gordo grabbed him around the neck.

And Gordo stuffed the preservation bot into its hopper, feet first.

"Kinda hoping…it would…do that…" Lyle2 said, smiling crookedly as the guardian tried to grind him up.

Face twitching, Lyle2 went down and down, till only his head showed. "Keesha…love…"

Keesha heard herself say, "Lyle… You keep leaving…"

The light went out in his remaining eye. Lubricants seethed from his mouth…

Gordo suddenly froze in place, with Lyle2's lifeless head sticking out of its hopper. Smoke rose from the grinders, wreathing the preservation bot's head. Gordo was hopelessly jammed by Lyle2's metal parts, as Lyle2 had hoped.

Gordo quivered, and slumped. Inert and broken.

Feeling achingly hollow, Keesha got to her feet and turned to find Curt on his knees, a few steps away. He was paper-pale with blood loss, clutching the submachine in one hand, pointing it shakily at her; he gripped the controller in his other hand. "Stay back or I'll cut you in half," he rasped. He was flicking the controller's levers…

And Black Betty responded, trundling obediently toward him. Keesha backed away, staring. Chuck was coming, too, rolling slowly along after Betty.

When the robot got close enough, Curt got agonizingly to his feet, groaning. He dropped the controller and the gun, then pulled himself up onto Black Betty's hopper. The robot lifted him up, turning him around—and eased his feet down into it—facing Keesha.

Curt grinned twitchily at her, as blood was squeezed out of his eyes and mouth…

"Sooner or later…" was all he managed to say before Black Betty ground his lungs into paste. His staring face disappeared into the robot. Its hopper closed.

That job done, Black Betty started automatically toward Keesha…

Keesha scooped up the controller, stopped Black Betty and Chuck in their tracks.

Then she sat down on the asphalt, and hugged her knees.

After a while, Keesha got up, walked slowly over to the burning wreckage of the bus, to see if anyone there was alive.

No. No one there at all, except a few decapitated corpses.

She made no sound as she walked slowly back to the box truck, though tears streamed from her eyes as if they had their own mission. Nothing to do with her.

How many had died in the bus?

She'd brought Curt here. Maybe it was her fault they'd died.

She'd been trying to help them. And now they were dead.

Good job, Keesha, you stupid bitch.

In the desert, beyond the gate, a little ways past the truck, she saw zombies, a large crowd of them, moving slowly toward the base.

Keesha's fingers seemed rubbery, so it was difficult to operate the controller. But she got the remaining robots moving, headed out to the gate. She set them up outside, on autonomous mode, to wait for the zombies.

The zombies came toward them—the robots went to meet them. Should keep them busy for a while.

Keesha went to the truck. She turned her back on the zombie-fueled guardians and got in the truck, drove it through the gate, put it in park, got out and locked the gate behind her.

She got back up in the box truck and drove it toward the dull gleam of Base 23. She drove slowly, twenty-five miles an hour, in case she ran into zombies.

She was headed for the gleaming metal of the old hangar. Might as well see if anyone she liked was still alive.

Numb, she thought. *Stay numb. That's what works.*

"I am the world's forgotten boy
The one who searches to destroy..."
— Iggy P*op*

I watched it going around and around, and I noticed the head turning to watch me as it came, and as it went.

ART OF DYING

"Searching for the truth among the lying
And answered when you've learned the
Art of Dying."
—*George Harrison*

I WAS WORKING ON my Carousel of Life & Death when my older brother Joe drove up in his big box truck. It was a hot, dusty day on the dry lake out in the Arizona desert. Wearing shorts, sandals and a sun hat, I was winding electric tape around the sculpture's power feed when the dusty gray truck rumbled up. I recognized the truck, so I didn't jump for my assault rifle leaning against the lever box.

I stared—then I waved, and turned back to the sculpture. The kinetic sculpture was squeaking and grinding as it turned. The broken bots from the robot graveyard were parading by on the circular platform, along with dead things; the dead dog, the headless robotic butler I'd put in that morning, they all swept regularly by, at a carousel's pace. There is no music to go with the sculpture's motion, unless you count the rhythmic squealing of its antiquated mechanism, sounding like a hoarse infant forever dying.

"Bunch of fags at the gate confiscated my guns," Joe growled, getting out of the truck, coughing the dust still pluming around it. He bared his teeth as he glanced angrily around—he still had all his teeth then…

I looked over at the other art encampments ranged around us, where sunburnt artists worked at ungainly constructs, half-shaped figures of metal, or in the shade of tents and pavilions, under bright colors muted by dust. "Don't call these people names," I told him. "Some of the folks here are gay—all of them are artists. None of 'em are fools. They're not going to let outsiders in the colony with weapons, Joe. Lotta bad roamers 'n raiders out there."

He gawped at my kinetic sculpture, eyebrows raised, taking a step back when the mummified dog came around as if it were rushing him. "Christ all-*fucking*-mighty," he swore. "What a waste of electronics, Perry!"

I grinned at him. He just shook his head.

My big brother Joe wasn't much like me. All we had in common was robots. (Which was pretty much all our parents had in common.) He was five years older, but I was a foot taller. He wore coveralls and a bulletproof vest. I wore as little as possible. He was thick-bodied, and stubby; his nose fat and broad like Dad's. I take after Mom so I'm slim and pale, with a nose like a hatchet blade. Joe and I have the same wiry brown hair and small eyes. He had something else different from me—a big smile, when he showed it, a whole lot of really large teeth. He was proud of it. Later, just before he died, I saw him on security cam without those teeth. The world took away his one point of vanity, and then it took everything else away from him…

I'D ONLY BEEN WORKING at the colony for a few months, since my folks died—if *died* is the word I want. I'd been fascinated by an old digital video of the annual art festivals they'd held up in the Nevada desert. Soon after the living dead started shambling around and gnoshing on brains—and before the so-called warbots began running around after them—a sudden incursion of braineaters brought the biggest desert art festival to a fitting Grand Guignol climax. The last big festival ended up with a bunch of stoned artists and the usual wannabes providing food for braineaters. I wonder if the zombies got a little high, eating those gray matter.

And then I heard about the "armed art colony." I made my way there as soon as I could, risking my life to get to a place where life might still mean something.

There are seven teams of artists and a few loners like me working out here—about forty total, now—including some cult types. (You know who you are, whatever you want to call that crap you're preaching.) And sometimes we get a few roamers who bring us what we need, mostly in exchange for…but you know what it's in exchange for. We have women here. They put up with it, but they make the roamers wash first.

I was pretty damned surprised when Joe showed up. The big galoot had sneered at the place when I told him about it. He'd been pissed off I wouldn't stay to help him run the robot graveyard—which he called Joe's Robotic Parts. But the robot graveyard is where Mom and Dad were over run; it's where the zombies got them both, when the electric fence failed. I hadn't been there when it happened, but I didn't want anything to do with the place. Or his stupid preservation bot.

"What brings you clear out here, Joe?" I asked, as the kinetic sculpture creaked rustily round and round.

He grunted. "You don't sound too thrilled to see me. I nearly got my ass overrun by braineaters coming out here." He glowered at the clumsily rotating sculpture. "You're all about this nonsense, at a time when nobody's got time for art." He spat at a scorpion scuttling under the sculpture. "Survival is all we've got time for now, man! There you go giving me that 'yeah, whatever' look of yours. Hell, I'm your goddamn brother, you glad to see me or *what?*"

"Sure, but if you think you're going to try to talk me into going back to the..."

He waved dismissively with a grease-stained hand. "I don't want you to be my partner anymore. I came out to tell you about our folks. And to make a deal with you. You know I need someone to do my preservation bot when I transfer into it, and the plain truth is I don't trust nobody with that but you. Help me and anything you want from the bot yard is yours."

"Still on the pres-bot trip? You Kurzweil guys never quit."

"It's the only way mankind is going to survive. If the zombies don't get us those lunatic warbots will—or sun-mad roamers."

"Sure, we're all survivalists now, but you're not trying to tell me something, are you? Cancer, maybe?" I couldn't figure why he'd want to try a transfer now; he never seemed suicidal before.

Joe laughed some and then spat on the ground. "Bro, I just need help around the yard is all, you not coming back. Might as well be myself, get it?"

It did have a sort of logic at that. I was glad he wasn't suicidal.

"Wait—what'd you say about our parents?"

He jammed his hands in his pockets. "Yeah, I spotted them in a shamble cluster about five miles east of the yard, in that gulley where you got this big piece of junk here. Or anyway, you know, I saw their bodies...walking around."

"Oh." We both knew what that meant. We'd have to go out there and try to shoot them from a safe distance. You didn't leave your parents' bodies walking around, thirsting for brains, eating human flesh. Disrespectful. And psychologically unbearable. You just couldn't get a decent night's sleep—till *they* were sent to the big sleep.

Me, I had gotten pretty skillful at not thinking about it. But it came up anyway, all the time, in my art.

"You in or not?" Joe asked.

"Yeah. I'm in. But..."

But it was dangerous as all hell to go out on a "re-killing expedition." I didn't want to admit to my macho brother that the trip scared me.

He was looking closer at my kinetic sculpture. The remains of a good-sized pit bull was rotating by. The dead dog was worked artfully into the sculpture, along with the robots and robotics parts I'd incorporated, and the skeleton of a man I'd found in the desert.

"This thing you made—it really is sick," he said, nodding toward the sculpture.

"Thanks."

"I didn't mean it as a fucking compliment."

I shrugged. "It's not done yet. Might make more sense to you later." But it probably wouldn't.

"Fucking merry-go-round with scary-ass bots and dead things on it. Crying out loud, Perry."

"It's not a merry-go-round, it's a kinetic sculpture, Joe." In fact the sculpture platform and some of the ride pistons, had once been part of an old cheaply made motorized carnival carousel, the portable kind that got trucked around to fairgrounds. A toothless old carny had tried to trade it to my dad at the robot graveyard. He'd turned the guy down and we found it later, dumped it in a gulley nearby. I almost got zombie-bit dragging it on sleds behind a truck to the yard.

It'd come with twelve splintery merry-go-round horses and other molded animals. I removed them all except one in the shape of a running wolf with a saddle on it—the human skeleton is riding the wolf now—and I replaced them with creaky old robots and bot shells and bits of corpses, engineered to shamble in place like zombies, or to seem to dance away from the braineater's grasp, as the platform turns. I spent eight months at the parts yard getting the engine going again, converting it to solar and giving the sculpture mind as well as motion. Then I'd trucked it out here. Mom had given me a ton of spare robot parts to take with me. "*May as well follow your bliss, son. Can't be any worse out there at that artists colony than it is here...*"

Follow your bliss. That's what she'd said. I loved my mom. She was the only one who tried to understand me. And Mom understood that my art is my salvation.

I've even gotten used to zombies through art. My art lets me say, *Yeah, this is the world now: Death is alive. The dead walk the Earth. Accept it. Celebrate it.*

But Joe turned away from my kinetic sculpture in disgust. "You got anything to drink?"

"Water."

"I've *got* water in the truck, Perry. Don't want any goddamn *water.*"

Joe sucked up liquor like a sponge; me, I don't like booze, I grow my own weed.

"Don't call me Perry around here. Or anywhere, if you want to get along with me." I don't like the cutesy sound of my own name: Perry Purvis. "In the colony I go by Puppeteer."

"*Puppeteer?* Figures."

"Anyway I don't have any booze right here. You want some weed?"

"Forget it, that stuff gives me the heebie-jeebies. I know one of your art-fag pals gotta have some liquor. I saw the stills cookin' cactus booze."

"Don't call them art fags, Joe."

"If they gimme some booze I'll call 'em fucking Picasso Da Vinci if they want."

TWO DAYS LATER JOE drove us through the desert, scouting for the ambulating remains of our parents in the gulley near the robot graveyard.

Braineaters go where brains are. Sometimes, sniffing for fresh, juicy gray matter, maybe frustrated by the depleted pickings around the city, a few zombies will wander out into the desert. After stumbling about for a while, they fall into a hole or slump from exhaustion and get their eyes pecked out by vultures—or they just dehydrate into living mummies. They're not able to move much, after dehydrating. They lay on the ground, half shriveled, like living roadkill. But even then there's a feverish spark in them; the zombie virus can still jumpstart the desiccated shreds of their nervous system.

The first zombies we saw were prostrate face-down and mummified by dehydration. Looking through the bug-splashed windshield of the slowly trundling box truck we saw several fallen zombies lying a few strides from each other in sandy open ground between purple sagebrush. At first they looked like empty clothes laid out to form bodies. But when we got out of the idling truck—wearing gloves and breathing masks in case of zombie blood spray, Joe with a double-barreled shotgun, me with my old AK—we saw the leathery brown mummified hands and feet sticking out from the tattered clothing; saw that their skullish heads were partly hidden by drifts of sand. They were "male" zombies, looked like.

Joe said something muffled through his mask. I pushed my breathing mask back onto the top of my head. "What'd you say?"

He pushed his mask back. "I said, I don't think it's them. Couldn't have dried out this much, this soon. Dammit, Perry, don't get that close."

"Puppeteer," I corrected him automatically, as I hunkered near one of the zombies. Sensing me close, its right hand trembled and contracted; the cords of its wasted jaw muscles contracted.

I stood up, stepped back, and shot the thing through the back of its head. My brother popped off the other two, one blast from each barrel of the 12 gauge.

He was visibly annoyed when I carried the light weight bundles of former people, one by one, to the back of the truck. He watched, cursing, as I stored them among some gunny sacks behind the cab.

"What the fuck, dude?"

"Parts for my sculpture," I said. "They don't take up much room."

"They still got the fucking virus in them!"

"I'm keeping my gloves on. And the virus'll die now that the fuckers are thoroughly dead. Come on, let's find what's left of..." I didn't want to actually say *Mom and Dad*.

We got back in the truck, drove on, over the bed of the gently winding gulley. We bumped along, driving over creosote bushes, crunching over the pitted trunks of fallen Joshua trees; over dead Manzanita that looked like driftwood from a lost ocean.

"Hey," Joe said, leering as he steered around a clump of flinty boulders, "you got some bitches at that art colony, right? I saw a couple, but they kept their distance. You get any of that tail?"

I winced and shook my head. "You *sure* I'm related to you?"

He laughed. "Come on, dude! They come across, at all? I'm in a real drought for pussy, here. It's been rough."

I sighed. "Truth is, those women sometimes make deals with roamers. You know, for stuff we need—food, ammo, antibiotics, like that.

Roamer's got to clean himself up first, and there's always a guard outside the tent to make sure he doesn't get rough. Sure, I guess they'd trade some sex to you, for something, if you followed the rules. But… I wouldn't want them to know my brother'd sink to that level. So don't tell them you're my brother."

"Hey, I *won't* tell 'em—'cause I want 'em to *like* me."

I blinked in the strobing of the sunlight as we drove in and out of shadows lengthening across the gulley, and tried to remember the last time I'd even thought about sex. Answer: a long time ago.

I'd learned not to think about it. The idea of copulation made me sick with horror. Sex involves congress with wet mouths and gaping body parts. I once saw a naked, nubile woman rush at a guy, her mouth open like she was going to give him a big wet kiss—and she *bit the guy's face off.* I couldn't have sex without imagining stuff like that. Any woman might be infected, since some people take longer than others to show it; she might change at any second into a thing that's sucking out my eyes so she can shove her tongue into my brain…

The truck lurched and so did my stomach.

We drove around boulders, a few clumps of tall cactus, then came to a draw that led like a ramp up onto the higher desert plains. "No sign of 'em…" Joe said, shaking his head. "Damn, I need a drink."

I was just thinking I needed to smoke some weed. I had that cramped, burnt feeling that meant I needed to smoke and chill out. But then, we might still see them. And I didn't want to be stoned when I saw my parents' bodies walking around.

We hit the old, cracked white concrete highway, and turned toward the robot graveyard. We were looking for a patchily overgrown gravel road that would take us back to Joe's compound.

That's when I saw the overturned RV. It was one of those really big hydrogen cell jobs, like a house driving around. The blue-and-white RV

The blue-and-white RV had flipped onto one side,
gray smoke wisping up from its engine.

had flipped onto one side, gray smoke wisping up from its engine. There were skid marks veering behind it, past the RV from us, the marks running right across two half-squashed, shattered, blood-soaked zombies. I could see neither one was Mom or Dad. As we drove closer we saw one of the road-smash zombies still thrashing. It was a naked fat guy separated into two parts, upper half waving fat blue arms, mouth spurting blood. Looked to me like the RV had plowed through a group of zombies on the road, blew out some tires, lost control, turned over. The impact as it fell on its side shattered windows in the back. The zombies would've climbed right in.

We drove a little closer, very slowly. Joe muttered, "Looks pretty recent, this happened."

"Who even drives an RV anymore? Where're they gonna vacation at?"

"I've seen that one—it was at that little truck stop, between the yard and town. That old trailer park."

"Uh-oh, here they come..."

Someone was crawling into view from behind the overturned RV. It was a teenage girl with blood-matted blond hair, face contorted with terror, dragging herself along with her arms. I could tell she wasn't a braineater—yet.

She crawled through broken glass, trying to get to our truck, screaming something at us, probably begging for help. The zombies came slowly but relentlessly after her, focused on their prey. I recognized the first zombie—it had been the white-haired Apache guy who'd run a shop at the truck stop. The braineater was creeping after her on all fours, broken bones angling from its lower calves.

The next zombie to shamble into view was the walking corpse of my father.

"Dad" was wearing the shreds of the mechanic's overalls he'd worn the day he'd gotten bit. His face was mostly gone on the right side, chewed away, along with one eye. But it was him, all right. He was chewing a gray gobbet of freshly ripped-out brain convolution, like a kid chewing jerky; it was hanging from the side of his mouth, waggling with his motions as he stalked along. He had his arms extended, clutching for the girl. I could see he'd broken a couple of fingers.

He? Or *it?* Usually I think of a zombie as *it*. Not always. It depends. Really, they have no gender, nor any personhood, anymore. But when it used to be your one of your parents...

Then came my mother, shambling onto the bloody concrete stage. Her face was blue; her lips were missing, raggedly excised. Her hands were blood-caked claws. She still wore her light blue sundress; holes torn in it, the hem smeared with offal. Her feet were bare, coated in filthy blood.

"Oh Jesus," Joe said hoarsely. "I didn't see 'em up this close before. Oh *fuck*." He looked warningly at me. "If you're gonna throw up, do it outside my truck...Puppeteer."

"Fuck you, Joe," I said, though I was close to vomiting. I plucked my AK47 from between the seats, opened the door, and climbed out into the hot dusk.

Out in the open, I could hear someone stuck in the RV wailing out a name, over and over, "Cindyyyyy! *Cindyyyyy!*" The zombies were hissing and gurgling; vultures screeched as they wheeled overhead. The girl was weeping and shrieking and babbling.

I pulled the breathing mask down over my face, grateful for the illusion of separation the goggles gave me, and flicked the rifle's safety off.

Joe was getting out on the other side of the truck, carrying the double-barreled shotgun. "I'll take Dad, you take Mom," he called.

Did he have to put it like that?

I walked slowly toward the zombies and the girl; toward the RV and the dying, the bloody broken glass and the living dead. It was all just about thirty feet away.

"Please," the girl rasped. "Kill them. I need help."

"Girl," my brother said, actual pity in his voice, "I'm sorry—but you got a big bite mark right on your face there. Surprised you still talking. Now I got to put you down..." He aimed the shotgun.

"No, no wait—I'm *not*—!" she quavered, crawling frantically toward him. The zombie on all fours grabbed one of her ankles and dragged her back. It bit into her broken calf so that her blood painted its face and her back arched with the pain. She jerked her leg away from the zombie, losing a chunk of calf. It let most of the raw flesh fall from its mouth—it's brains they really want.

Joe was licking his lips, hands shaking as he drew a bead on her.

"No, mister, *don't—!*"

"Joe...?" I'm not sure what I was going to say. I felt like I should speak up for her. But how could I? If he didn't shoot her, I'd have to.

Joe fired and blew the top of her head off, splashing brain matter over the zombie clutching at her ankle. As the girl went limp, the braineater growled and stuck its gray tongue out to lick the bits of her spattered brains off its lips—maybe licking up her memories, her dreams. Grunting, it began to lick jellied brains off the back of her leg...

I shot it in the head, a *good* shot punching through the thing's left temple. Most everyone alive is pretty good at head shots. That's why they're still alive.

Mom and Dad...their shambling bodies...were just a few steps past the dead girl. They were coming at us, arms outstretched in hideous parody of loving parents reaching out to embrace their children.

My mother's dead body looked at me through milky eyes. I thought I saw...probably imagined...a glint of recognition in those dead white eyes. Maybe there was a little flickering memory in there—but still her fingers clutched and her mouth snapped at me.

Still—I couldn't shoot, not yet.

She was shambling closer. Almost within reach.

"Mom…" I said.

"Don't be an asshole," Joe said, reloading the shotgun. "Shoot her! It's not *them!*"

He aimed, fired at Dad, the first round blowing through the sternum, the second shattering my father's face; exploding his head.

I looked back at Mom just as she lunged at me and grabbed the barrel of my AK—and it seemed to me she pulled its muzzle against her chest. I squeezed the trigger and she was blown backwards. Blood splashed the assault rifle, runneled down it, spiraling toward my gloved hands.

Instinctively, I dropped the gun, afraid the blood would run past the gloves, get on my skin, maybe insinuate into some forgotten abrasion.

Mom's body was still living, arms flapping, moving almost like a swimmer doing the back stroke on the dry, dusty concrete.

"You dumbass," Joe muttered, reloading. He sidled over to me, aimed his gun down at Mom and shot her through the eye—only one round. But it was enough.

My mother's living corpse shuddered and stopped moving, her body relaxing. Something went limp inside me too, then. My knees went rubbery, and I almost fell over.

Joe grabbed my arm and shoved me against the grill of the truck. "Get your feet under you! More of 'em coming!"

Zombies were coming from around the back of the RV; a group of them, maybe six. There was a braineater in unidentifiably fouled rags, dragging one leg, missing his jaw; a zombie in a bloody party dress walked beside the first like his companion to a cannibal party; there was a badly decayed Mestizo zombie, and a small naked braineater who'd been a kid of maybe twelve. And there were others coming behind those.

Joe broke down his shotgun, checked his pockets. "Dammit, I'm outta ammo! The rest is in the truck! Use your AK!"

"I'm not touching that thing, man!"

The zombies were moving a little faster now, as if smelling our vulnerability.

"Come on, Perry, you dumb fuck, you're wearing gloves!"

"Just get in the truck," I told him, "and open the back! Make the ramp come down!"

He shot me a look of puzzlement but got up in the cab of the truck, and hit the button opening the rear. The door of the freight box hummed upward as I grabbed Mom's body by the ankles and towed what was left of her toward the back of the truck. I dragged her dead weight up the loading ramp, into the truck, dropped her and ran past her, jumped out the back.

Joe was yelling something angry at me, I couldn't make out what, as I ran around to the front of the truck.

The zombies were a few shuffling steps from Dad's body.

"Goddammit, what the fuck are you *doing!*" Joe yelled. He was gunning the truck engine, as if it were roaring at me too.

"I'm not leaving them! Their bodies have got to be taken care of!"

I grabbed the ankles of my father's corpse, and towed it to the back of the truck, terrified I was going to stumble and fall. I might not be able to get up before they were on me. I dragged Dad's body up the ramp, yelling at Joe, *"Go! Run 'em over and let's go!"*

The truck jolted forward and I almost pitched onto Dad's body. I grabbed a wall stud in the back of the truck, managed to keep my feet as the vehicle swerved. I steadied as the truck roared down the road, then pulled the bodies of my parents deeper into the freight box. The ramp, still extended, scraped on the road, spitting sparks.

Looking out the open rear door I saw the zombies mindlessly trooping after the truck. Joe had driven around them.

Ten minutes of riding with the shattered bodies of my parents and then we hit the gravel road off the old highway, and turned, headed toward the junkyard.

We got there in another twenty minutes of me coughing with dust, trying not to look at the bodies of my mom and dad lying at my feet…

Joe opened the gate of the yard with his remote, drove past the fried remains of several zombies cooked by the electric fence, and into the loading area, quickly closing the gate behind us. When he pulled up I jumped out and ran to where he was climbing down from the cab. "Why didn't you run them over? They're likely to follow us here!"

"I'm not getting zombie gore all over the front of my truck, goddammit!" he snapped. "The shit might drip on me when I get out, and anyway I'd have to use good water washing off the grill…" He seemed coldly furious as he closed the gate and stumped off toward his bunker. "You deal with those bodies! I can't stand to look at 'em no more." He was mad about what happened to our folks; he was mad because he'd had to shoot holes in their bodies. He was mad at me because I was the only person around to be mad at.

"Sure," I said. "I'll take care of it. Whatever."

As the sun set, I sprayed the back of the box truck with anti-viral foam, soaking my parents' bodies and the mummified zombie roadkill too. I waited till the foam subsided, then I got a sealant gun, sprayed them all with a light coating of latex to slow rot, flipped them over, sprayed them again.

When the latex dried I dragged the bodies of my folks, Dad first, down the ramp, across the loading area, past the old solar-powered light-blue Ford pickup Mom used to drive. I tucked them both out of sight behind the rusting hulk of a broken street-sweeper bot. I stowed the mummified dead zombies behind an old robot enforcer chassis.

Relieved, I cleaned up, threw away my gloves, then went to sit on the passenger-side running board of the box truck, where I smoked a joint and watched the fading light change colors; I could see dust whirling in the neon-orange sunset glow; the dust was turning, settling, with aching slowness.

WHEN I WOKE UP the next morning, Joe was doing maintenance on the box truck, muttering that he was going to take it to the compound south of Tucson, do some trading. He'd put together a stash of old pharmaceuticals to barter for bot parts—and liquor. "You want to be helpful, prep that second preservation bot—it's my backup, mostly just a head right now. You'll find it in the tool shed."

"I'm supposed to deal with their bodies on my own?"

"Yeah. You didn't want to keep their business going. So you can do that for them. Bury 'em wherever the hell you want."

He still seemed pissed off, frowning and silent as he opened the gates, with me standing by with a rifle. I didn't see any zombies.

And Joe drove off in his big truck, without another word, closing the gate behind him with his remote. That was the last time I saw him alive, except on the security footage.

I looked over the second pres-bot in the workshop. It would need work to make it fully receptive to a mind imprint. Checking the holofiles, it looked to me like Joe had tried to copy his mind onto it—the bot's drive already had some stuff on it called "Joseph Purvis." He didn't get that much on there. I didn't have the gear at the yard to make it work. I knew a guy at the colony who might be able to do it, with some convincing; preservation bots were a big point of contention for most. But a promise is a promise, so I decided to take it back there in Mom's old pickup—

with the bodies of my parents, too. There was a small cemetary in the colony. I'd bury them there, where I could visit their graves.

I wrapped their bodies in tarps, and carried them over my shoulder to the back of the pickup. I put the head of the secondary preservation bot in bubble wrap—I thought I caught a malicious glare in its realistic glass eyes as I stowed it in the back of the pickup between what was left of my parents. Almost as an afterthought I stacked the three mummified zombies in the back, to one side of my parents, one zombie atop the next.

Then I dug into some of my brother's freeze-dried stores. After choking down some pseudo eggs, I climbed up into the watchtower, and looked out over the robot graveyard, past the piles of electronic scrap, and the high electric fences to the desert. A group of shambling figures cast long shadows in the morning light, about sixty yards out there—but they were off the gravel road, a good ways, seemed to be worrying at some dead creature, perhaps a coyote, in a clump of cacti. They weren't in close to the gates.

The time to go was right now, I decided, as I climbed down to the junkyard. My brother would be gone for five or six days. If he went on a bender in a compound, he'd be gone longer. I'd have time to bury my parents, fix the back-up preservation bot, and get back here to deliver it to him—and maybe if I fixed the bot he'd let me sort through the robot scrap to find some gear I could use in my art.

Joe had cleaned up the AK and taken it with him. A shotgun clipped along the window behind me, I drove the pickup to the gate, used my mother's remote control, clipped to the pickup visors, to open it. I waited, and watched, as the gate rolled open. No movement out there. The zombies I'd spotted were a fair distance away. I had the shotgun. Why was I hesitating? A *frisson* of mindless fear seemed to freeze my hands to the steering. Maybe it was a premonition.

Finally I forced myself to put the pickup in gear, and I drove it out into the desert.

I pressed the remote as I drove through, so the gate would shut right behind me. I heard it rolling...

I thought I heard another sound, a kind of popping noise. I glanced at the rearview. Was the gate moving kind of shudderingly?

The zombies were there, suddenly, on the road ahead. I could mow several of them down with the pickup—but the others might grab on, as I passed, smash at the windows...

I veered to the left, offroad, bumping over rocks and sage, then angling back to the road when I was safely past. I wasn't feeling confident enough to skeet-shoot a large group of zombies with my shotgun.

I slowed, glanced back toward Joe's Robotics. I couldn't see the gate from here. It was closed, wasn't it? It *had* closed—hadn't it?

To be sure it was closed, I'd have to go back through the cluster of zombies again...

I shrugged my doubt away. It must have closed all the way. Stop worrying, Puppeteer...

I MADE IT UNBITTEN to the art colony and I got caught up in things there. Burying my folks, first—I laid them out together, in one shallow grave. It was hard to shovel dirt over their bodies but I was relieved when it was over and done.

Then I got hung up working on the preservation bot. The bearded, almost perpetually silent computer artist who called himself Smegma helped me with it, as I'd hoped—but it was a slow process. We had no way to order spare parts. No electronics store to visit.

Finally I got the bot running. I sat on the ground in my work shed, near the kinetic sculpture, and held the vaguely Joe-like head in my lap, and I switched it on. Its eyes lit up—it seemed angry, scowling. Accusatory.

"What the fuck, bro?" it said, its voice warping. "What the fuck, bro?"

"Well, sounds like you, anyway." I chuckled over that. "Still mad at me, for no good reason." I switched it off and the next morning I was just stowing it in the back of the truck, swaddled in bubble wrap, when the raiders came.

The raiders were old "friends": the Red Face bunch, faces painted red—we'd driven them away three times already. They'd come back once more, with a new tactic.

I was just wedging the bot's head in place between some crates of homemade liquor for Joe when I heard the roar of a powerful engine, and a siren blaring—the siren was probably to put a scare in us—and then the eastern inner fence imploded. A bot-driven dump truck backed through in a rising cloud of red dust, smashing a long stretch of fence into flinders. Then the dump truck stopped, making that beep-beeping sound they make, and its bed tilted up—and dumped. The raider had somehow herded twenty zombies into the back of a dump truck and they backed it up to our compound fences, smashed through, dumped the zombies right into our colony. And then, laughing, they drove away.

The zombies were supposed to drive us out of the colony, I guess—and they almost did. But we held the line. The braineaters moved with surprising speed, killing a half-dozen startled, stoned artists, including one of our few females. But everyone here is proficient at head shots and never far from a weapon. Instead of doing a runner, leaving the colony with the zombies chasing us—the way the raiders had figured it—we stuck around, ducking behind our own artwork for cover, and killed the zombies. Of course, afterwards, we had to kill a couple of our own who'd gotten bitten…

But the Red Face raiders were still out there, once the battle was done, and the fences, outer and inner, were still breached. We drove the bloodthirsty pricks back—but a long siege followed during which we nearly starved to death. We got pretty desperate. Some of the artists were looking at other artists the way hungry zombies look at brainfood.

Finally we formed our own raiding party, took the fight to the raiders, using rifles and Molotovs made from the best stuff out of our stills—firebombs of pure alcohol—and drove them off.

But it was a long time before any of us felt safe enough to leave the colony. Months.

Finally, I decided to risk it. I set off one morning, driving back to Joe's Robotics, the preservation head beside me on the floor of the passenger's side. It was a long trip and a dangerous one. Any movement outside an armed compound was dangerous. Just before I left, I tried to talk Smegma into going with me.

He silently shook his head. After a moment he said, in a voice hoarse with disuse, "But good luck."

I GOT TO JOE'S place about an hour before sunset. The gate of the robot graveyard was closed, which was good. No sign of the zombies.

It took me three tries to get the remote in Mom's pickup to open the gate. Finally it rattled open…

Inside, I found the yard deserted. But there were old, dried splashes of blood in the loading area and a pile of dust mixed with bits of bone and rotting flesh.

Feeling sick, I checked the bunker. The primary preservation bot was gone. So was a lot of other stuff. Food, water, primo electronics.

I felt dread like a heavy chunk of shrapnel, jagged and heavy in my chest.

Then I remembered Joe's surveillance system, the hidden cameras he'd set up to watch the gate from inside. Joe was a stone survivalist, and never missed a trick.

I found the surveillance unit in the bunker, and rolled back the footage, too far at first so that I saw myself driving out through the open gate, seen from inside the yard; saw the gate closing…and saw it jolt to a stop before it was fully closed. A puff of smoke was rising from the gate mechanism. The gate reversed, then, opening up again. And stayed that way. Wide open.

Oh, shit.

So either Mom's old controller or some short in the system had kept the gate open behind me. I'd *thought* there might've been something wrong. But I'd been too cowardly to go back and check.

Hands shaking, I advanced the surveillance file till I saw intruders. First came the zombies, shuffling into the yard, sniffing around. Not long after came another set of intruders: human outsiders, in a dirt buggy. There were three people in the dusty vehicle: a black woman, a black man, both fairly young, maybe siblings, and a grubby-looking white guy.

They got out, and were immediately hunted by the zombies. The outsiders were efficient at killing braineaters; made pretty short work of them. Then they got the gate closed, and went into the bunker.

Advancing the footage, I worked out that one of them seemed to have killed another—the white guy'd shot the young black guy. The black woman got some justice for that, aired out the white guy, dumped his body unceremoniously outside the fence. Now she was alone. She put the body of her brother, if that's who he was, out in the loading area.

I advanced the footage some more, and she was no longer alone—the preservation bot appeared, at her side, re-shaped to resemble the dead black kid. Probably with his personality imposed on it. She made the bot bury the kid's body: a strange sight that seemed to have some kind of wider meaning…

Then a new outsider showed up, climbing over the fence, insulating himself from the electrics.

I saw them confront him…and he talked his way in.

Almost ran out of video after that, with a long dull period passing—then I saw them testing the big robots they'd built, a kind I'd never seen before. The electronics artist in me watched in fascination as they did preliminary tests. I couldn't see what they'd done with them out into the desert…But when they returned, the bots were smeared with blood and gore.

The test was over; the girl, the killer robots, and the new guy stood around in the loading area, and suddenly the gate opened—and Joe drove through in his box truck.

He got out and confronted them. I don't know exactly what was said. I saw that Joe had lost most of his teeth. Probably got into a fight with a raider. He tried to take the yard back, by force. That was stupid, Joe. You were outnumbered.

And he didn't know what the robots were capable of…

Then the new white guy directed a monster robot, on treads, to grab Joe; to stuff him into a hopper in its mid section; to grind him up.

They ground my brother up *alive*, in a huge, semi-intelligent meat grinder on wheels…

Soon after that, they left in the box truck. I don't know where they went. There's no way I can find them. The best I can do is try to remember what happened to Joe, to my whole family. And do it my way…

So I returned to the colony. And I wrote this account, which I'm going to include in my sculpture, locked away inside it, a sort of time capsule.

But the real truth, the real *accounting*—is in the sculpture itself.

• • •

Video Presentation on Puppeteer Final Installation: Puppeteer and Family

Hello! Glad you could join us out here at the Low Desert Colony for the Arts. If the viddy is a little grainy, hey, I feel like that fits. What we need to see, clearly and sharply, is the dance of death in the machine of life. As the kinetic installation turns, you'll see my presentation. It'll be right there on the screen mounted on the fixed center pole of the installation, and you'll hear the story unfold....

I decided to film this presentation when I saw what happened to my brother, Joseph Purvis. The voice you're hearing now belongs to Puppeteer Purvis.

What prompted the final stage of this sculpture was the death of my brother Joe. I had a hard time accepting the way my brother died, at first. When I watched him being crushed, smashed, splashed, killed—as you see in this clip I took from the surveillance footage—I tried to tell myself it wasn't real. People don't die that way. People aren't eaten by robots. People are eaten by zombies. They don't die like Joe did.

But it's real, all right. And maybe it was inevitable. First the robots, then the virus, then this...

Zombies. Robots. All part of one great tableau. And I'm there, too—reconciling it all through art.

Let's look at the *finale* to my brother's life, once more...

And there you see it, on video—his death. Hideously undignified, unspeakably agonizing.

My brother, Joe Purvis, was not an easy man to live with, but it was cruel, having to watch him die that way, especially hard knowing that it was probably my fault. I'd left the gate open.

Completing my sculpture, I installed the robotic semblance of Joe—that's his angry face you see sweeping by, on the stocky capering mechanical figure there. I've even dressed the body in a pair of his coveralls. When I first installed "Joe" into the sculpture and switched on the platform, I watched it going around and around, and I noticed the head turning to watch me as it came, and as it went. As it came and as it went; as it came and as it went...

Sometimes I could feel hatred burning from its glass eyes. You can feel it too, as you watch it go by.

Right after the semblance of Joe, you'll see the re-animated bodies of my parents. I dug them up—found them fairly well preserved by the latex spray. Do you see them, there, rotating by? I did a kind of crude taxidermy on them so their bodies are mostly hollow, but I've got old-school animatronic-style machinery in them, making their limbs move, helping them perform a slow dance around one another. Then it goes into its second mode, and they behave like zombies, reaching for me; then they're back to behaving like dancing people, then like zombies, reaching...

Reaching for me. That's me, there, you're seeing, by now—I'm between the preserved bodies of my parents, and Joe's secondary preservation bot, just past the wolf ridden by the skeleton and the leaping pit bull, the dead dog going up and down, up and down, and the three mummified zombies who're now trying to catch my family, chasing us, never quite catching us; their skeletons partly replaced with machine parts, their hands animatronically clutching.

Around and around it goes and you see me again, just a part of the kinetic sculpture. Finding my place at last. I don't mind dying to complete the sculpture. My friend Smegma understood—he will have sprayed me with preservative, once I'm in place, to keep me from too much rot. He'll hose off the worst of the mess, too, and he'll maintain this work of art for me.

As I record this, I haven't yet thrown the switch that will make me part of the sculpture forever. But if you watch the video you'll see me throw the switch. You'll see the spike come up from below, to impale me through the anus, to stab straight and true, inexorably upward; to penetrate my body, up through my throat and punch out the top of my head. I've set it all up very carefully and tested it on a "volunteer" raider we caught.

I want to thank the colony for its encouragement and cooperation in the creation of this unique work of art.

Thanks to their assistance, you should now be watching my impaled body riding round and round, up and down, on the merry-go-round piston, my arms flapping in a kind of awkward dance—an absurd, chaotic dance that sums up my life so well.

As you watch on the video accompanying the sculpture, you'll see me do penance for what happened to Joe; for all of humanity, really. For all of us—for letting the world come to this: a dance of robots, zombies, and the hapless fools trapped between them…

And now I'm ready to become part of a work of art.

Now—I will throw the switch.

Let there be art!

"I'm damaged, and I like it:
It made me what I am…"

— B*lue* Ö*yster* C*ult,*
C*urse of the* H*idden* M*irror*,
lyric by J*ohn* S*hirley*.

SOME WOULD SAY ZOMBIES are even now the norm, that the zombies are our neighbors, our politicians, our business leaders living their sleepwalking lives—but they don't eat live human brains directly...our brains are eaten by certain media, by reality shows and political action committee programming and the worst of the internet. But given a world in which literal zombies are unfortunately extant, and in which robots are ubiquitous, how do we combine them interestingly?

That question sparked the main idea behind "Food Chain." The main idea behind its prequel/sequel combination, "Art of Dying," is that in order to live with a world of horror, art must find a way to reconcile us with it. Perhaps madness is the only reconciliation left...

—John Shirley,
June 06, 2012